Shadow of Doubt

By Jeremy Brown

Scholastic

New York   Toronto   London   Sydney
Mexico City   New Delhi   Hong Kong   Buenos Aires

No part of this publication may be reproduced in whole or in part, stored in a retrieval system, or transmitted in any form or by any means, electronic, mechanical, photocopying, recording, or otherwise, without written permission of the publisher. For information regarding permission, write to Scholastic Inc., Attention: Permissions Department, 557 Broadway, New York, NY 10012.

ISBN 0-439-76935-3

Design by Steve Scott

12 11 10 9 8 7 6 5 4 3 2 1   6 7 8 9 10 11/0
Printed in the U.S.A.
First printing, June 2006

Table of Contents

PERSONNEL FILE

CSI Wes Burton: Burton is a witty, intelligent investigator who loves the problem-solving nature of crime scene investigation. His signature fly fisherman's vest, bristling with evidence-gathering tools, is a welcome sight at any crime scene (except those run by Detective Gibson). Not much surprises Burton, including a criminal's ability to weave a nearly perfect lie. He usually prefers evidence analysis to talking with witnesses and suspects because, unlike people, "evidence stands up; it does not lie." He appreciates Detective Radley's interviewing skills and her interest in *why* a crime occurred, because it allows him to focus on the *how*.

Detective Erin Radley: At six-foot-one, Detective Radley can be an intimidating woman. Her motto, "Convict them with kindness," seems in conflict with her physical appearance, but it is that contradiction that keeps suspects off balance and talking to her. When a woman of her stature hands you a blanket and hot chocolate, then asks why you stabbed your wife, it's hard to concentrate on your lie. Radley has a master's degree in psychology and tends to focus on the *why* of a case. She plans to publish a study someday on what compels criminals to commit their crimes. Working with Burton presents plenty of odd situations that will help her book stand out. She appreciates Burton's dedication to solving crimes and his ability to lighten situations that most individuals would find disturbing and depressing.

Detective Frank Gibson: Gibson is what he would call "old school," using intimidation and a loud voice to get a confession rather than patience and by-the-book techniques. In some cases his approach is required, such as when a kidnapper won't divulge the location of his latest victim, but for the most part Burton and his team do not appreciate Gibson's presence at a crime scene. Gibson and Burton constantly clash with each other, and when it comes to solving a crime, they have an unspoken competition to see who can identify the perpetrator first. The perps don't stand a chance.

Mike Trellis: Trellis is Burton's CSI technician assistant. He specializes in trace analysis, arson, and horrible jokes, such as commenting that a shooting victim died from "Too much lead in his diet." It doesn't help that he follows every joke with "Get it?" Burton knows that when Trellis is working on a case, he can expect close attention to detail, exhaustive analysis of evidence, and dedication to finding the guilty party. Detective Gibson likes to pick on Trellis, but the young technician has a knack for frustrating the burly cop, and for that, Burton likes him even more.

Lauren Crown: Dr. Crown is a shy, almost reclusive forensic pathologist. A genius in her field, she is nearly incapable of having a normal conversation. However, she is quick to recite the qualifications of a forensic pathologist[1] should any-one refer to her as a medical examiner, or worse, a coroner. She can determine a corpse's time of death within ten min-utes just by looking at it, but she has no idea who the president of the United States is — and doesn't care.

Ed: Ed, short for Exhibit D, is a search-and-rescue border collie. She was adopted and trained by Burton after being admitted as evidence in a case against her owner, a metham-phetamine dealer. Her fur contained trace elements of the ingredients used to make crystal meth, and the dealer was convicted. She can follow ground and air scent and is in training to become a certified cadaver dog as well.

Burian U. Gorlach: Burian, or Bug, as he prefers to be called, is a Russian immigrant and the owner of Sensitive Cleaners, a company that cleans and decontaminates crime scenes when an investigation is complete. Bug is anything but sensi-tive, muttering in semi-English and cackling while he rips up bloodstained carpets and vacuums biohazards.

---

[1] As a physician who specializes in the investigation of sudden, unex-pected, and violent deaths, the forensic pathologist attempts to determine the identification of the deceased, the time of death, the manner of death (natural, accident, suicide, or homicide), the cause of death, if the death was by injury, and the nature of the instrument used to cause the death, using methods such as toxicology, firearms examination (wound ballistics), trace evidence, forensic serology, and DNA technology.

The Breath of Death

CSI Wes Burton walked into the interview room and saw the suspect, Josh Lorion, sitting at the table. In the corner, as far away from Lorion as he could get, Detective Frank Gibson popped another piece of gum in his mouth.

"What's the problem?" Burton said. "Did Lorion scare you away?"

"He didn't," Gibson said, "his dragon breath did. The guy must have eaten ten onions to get that stench."

"Not ten," Lorion said. "Just half of one, though it was quite potent. I still have the other half at home if you'd like some."

"How can you eat onions for breakfast?" Gibson said, his face contorted.

"I didn't," Lorion said. "I had it with dinner last night. I just haven't had a chance to brush my teeth yet. Besides, sometimes it's nice to let the taste of an onion linger."

"You've got problems, buddy," Gibson said. "Even though you're here in connection with a murder case, I ought to put you in jail for assaulting an officer with your stink mouth."

"I didn't kill anybody," Lorion said.

Burton sat down across from him. "Right now, that's an opinion. I'm going to find out whether it's a fact or a lie."

"Burton, you want some gum?" Gibson said from the corner. Burton got his first whiff of the onion smell coming from Lorion and extended his hand for a piece. He popped it in his mouth while he reviewed the file. Lorion sighed, bringing a moan from Gibson.

"Okay," Burton said. "I'm going to tell you what we know. If at any time you'd like to interrupt me to confess, feel free." Lorion gave him a blank look. "Here we go: A female body was found in the woods along Rural Route 657 this morning. The body hasn't been dead long, probably since 10 P.M. last night. A witness reported a car that matches yours was driving slowly down Rural Route 657 at approximately 1 A.M."

"It is illegal to take a drive at night?" Lorion said.

"Now, see," Burton said. "I told you it was okay to interrupt me to confess. Anything else is going to have to wait until I'm done." Lorion didn't like that, but Burton didn't care. "Do you want to confess?"

"Not quite," Lorion said.

"Come on, man," Gibson said. "I need to air this place out. At least the jail cell has a small window."

"That's funny," Lorion said. "Ha ha ha!" He blew each fake laugh in Gibson's direction.

"That's it," Gibson said, coming out of the corner. "You ever use Drano as mouthwash?"

"Frank, please," Burton said. "If he gets nervous, he'll start breathing faster, and no one wants that." Gibson settled back into his corner and chomped his gum. "Now, Mr. Lorion, what were you doing last night?"

6

"I ate my dinner, watched some TV, and when I couldn't get to sleep, I went for a drive," Lorion said.

"Who was with you?" said Burton.

"No one," Lorion said. "I was alone."

"With that breath, I'm not surprised," said Gibson. There was a knock on the door, and CSI technician Mike Trellis leaned in.

"Wes, I have the results from the autopsy and *whoa, what is that smell, I gotta get out of here!*" Trellis slammed the door, and the three men in the interview room could hear him hacking in the hallway.

"I'll be right back," Burton said.

"I'll come with you," said Gibson. Burton would have been surprised since Gibson took every chance to be alone with a suspect, but the onion smell was becoming unbearable. In the hallway, Trellis was at the drinking fountain trying to rinse out the inside of his nose.

"What did you and Dr. Crown find, Mike?" Burton asked.

"Oh, man," Trellis said, wiping his face on his sleeve. "What did that guy eat? Hot garbage?"

"Half an onion," Gibson said. "Imagine if he'd had the whole thing."

"Onion?" said Trellis. He flipped through the autopsy report, blinking tears out of his eyes so he could read it. "We found onion in the stomach of the dead woman. She must have eaten it just before she died, because it was pretty intact."

"That's a nice coincidence," Gibson said, "but it doesn't prove Lorion killed her. Lots of people had onion last night."

"I can prove whether it's a coincidence or not," Burton said. "I just need a warrant for half an onion."

Why did Burton want the other half of the onion?

Burton's File

All living things have DNA, including stinky onions. By comparing the DNA of the onion found in the dead woman's stomach to the DNA of Lorion's remaining half onion, the lab can determine if she was at his home the night she was murdered.

A Fresh Coat of Murder

Bug was waiting outside the warehouse when Burton and Mike Trellis pulled up. He was wearing a white Tyvek jumpsuit, and the loose fit made him look like a marshmallow man. He waved at them with both hands.

"He'd make a great mascot," Trellis said from the passenger seat.

"Except for those brown stains on his suit," said Burton. "They could be dried blood."

Trellis said, "Why else would he call us? What else is brown and requires a professional cleaner?" It didn't take long to come up with an answer.

"Oh, no," they both said.

Outside the truck, they walked toward Bug. He was the only one smiling.

"Hello, Burtons and Mikes!" he said. "Welcome to crime scene!"

"Are you sure this is a crime scene?" Burton said.

"What's that on your suit?" Trellis said, wanting to know right away.

"This?" Bug said as he swiped a finger through a stain on his stomach.

"Oh, no." The CSIs groaned again.

"This is paint," said Bug. "The man inside, Garys, moved into warehouse last week and decided to make it look nice before boxes arrive. I say to him, 'Why brown?' and he say back, 'Brown hides dirt.'"

"The man has a point," Trellis said.

"Ah, but Mikes, what else hides dirt?" Bug asked, leaning in.

"Darkness?" Trellis said.

"Wrong! Brooms!" said Bug. "You clean the dirt, you don't hide the dirt. You don't want to sweep, you call Sensitive Cleaners."

"So did Gary call you?" Burton said.

"No, Burtons," said Bug. "And his name is Garys, not Gary. Garys just rents warehouse, it is owned by another man. He hires me to check for problems every season. I am patrolling for sign of insects, and I find stain on floor that looks like blood."

"Lots of things can look like blood," Burton said. "Grease, oil, ketchup . . ."

"Brown paint," Trellis said.

"Please," Bug said. "I have cleaned all kinds of stains. I do not see paint and call it blood. And besides, it tastes funny."

"You tasted the stain?" Burton said while Trellis tried to keep his breakfast down.

"What? No, I must have it wrong," Bug said. "Something is strange here. Not taste . . . feel! It feels funny."

"Got it," Burton said, letting out a breath.

Bug pulled a barf bag out from somewhere and handed it to Trellis. "Save me trouble," he said. "Do not mess on floor."

"It's in the bag," Trellis said. "Get it? Because I'll puke in the bag."

"I get it!" Bug said. "Bah ha ha ha!" Burton was inside the warehouse by the time Bug stopped laughing.

"Are you Gary?" Burton said, walking toward a man with a clipboard.

"Garys, yes," the man said.

Burton stopped. "Your name is really *Garys*?"

"Is there a problem?" Garys said.

"No, it's just that . . . never mind. I'm Wes Burton, with the crime lab. We're here to check out a suspicious stain."

"Which one?" Garys said. "The last company to rent this space must have dumped all their garbage on the floor and stomped on it. I'm having the whole surface repainted next week."

"Looks like you've already done a nice job on the walls," Burton said.

"Yeah," said Garys. "The place hadn't seen a fresh coat in years."

"We'll check out the stain and will hopefully be out of your way shortly," Burton said. He walked toward Trellis and Bug, who were standing near the corner against the back wall.

"What do you see?" Burton asked Trellis.

"Could be blood," the technician said, crouching next to the stain on the floor.

"Time for a quick test," said Burton as he pulled a small spray bottle of fluorescein out of vest pocket 23.

"What is this?" Bug said.

"This is fluorescein," Burton said. He sprayed the thick liquid on part of the floor stain and the freshly painted wall above it. "I'll shine my ultraviolet light on it when I'm done spraying. If it glows, that means blood is present. I like to use it first instead of luminol, which does the same thing. They both have pros and cons. Luminol won't detect traces of blood if chlorine bleach has been used to clean it, but it can expose blood that has been painted over. Fluorescein won't do that."

"Gather around, guys," Burton said. "I need you to block out as much light as possible." He snapped on his handheld UV light from vest pocket 25, and the stain fluoresced.

"Gentlemen, we have blood," Burton said.

"Interesting pattern," said Trellis. "Lots of spatter and droplets. It seems like there should be more blood, maybe on the wall."

"I agree," Burton said, pulling a bottle of luminol out of vest pocket 23. He misted the liquid over another area of the floor stain and again up onto the wall above it. Trellis brought the UV light in close.

"No glow on the floor this time," Burton said, "but the wall shows blood spatter and handprints."

"What does this mean?" Bug said.

"It means Garys is trying to cover a murder with his brown paint," Burton said.

How did Burton know it was Garys who covered the blood and not the previous tenant?

Burton's File

The blood on the floor glowed with fluorescein, which can detect blood that's been cleaned with chlorine bleach but not blood that's been painted over. The blood on the wall glowed with luminol, which can expose blood that's been painted over but not if it's been cleaned with chlorine bleach. So, the floor was cleaned with bleach, and the wall was painted over. Since Garys said the place hadn't seen a fresh coat of paint in years, he had to have seen the bloodstain before he painted over it.

A Gut Feeling for Guilt

Burton followed Mike Trellis into the crime lab and found Detective Frank Gibson talking with Dr. Lauren Crown. They were standing on opposite sides of the body of Carol Green, which had been dropped off about a half hour ago.

"We can't hold her husband for much longer," Detective Gibson said as Burton and Trellis approached. "We need to find out how she died before we let him go."

"The autopsy process cannot be rushed," Crown explained, speaking slowly. "If there is something particular you'd like me to look for, a suspected cause of death, perhaps I can check that first."

"Yeah," Gibson said. "Look for a note from her husband that says 'I killed my wife.'"

"That's usually in the spleen," Burton said, standing next to Dr. Crown. "Right next to the neon sign that says 'Gibson is an idiot.'"

"Fantastic," said Gibson. "Two more nerds to stand around and not give me any information."

"I'm not a nerd," Trellis said. "I'm a geek."

"My apologies," said Gibson.

"What's the story here?" Burton said. "You think Mr. Green killed his wife, but you can't prove it yet?"

"Pretty much," Gibson said. "According to Mr. Green, they went out for dinner at the Primo Pasta Palace around six o'clock last night, then went dancing at the Boogie Barn from 8:30 until 11:30. He says they got into an argument when it was time to leave, and he ended up walking home. He strolled around for a few hours to cool off and got home around 1 A.M. He says he found his wife, dead, in the garage."

"Did any witnesses see them?" Burton asked.

"We have conflicting accounts," Gibson said. "Some people saw them, some didn't. They weren't out with friends, so there isn't anyone who recognized them. We do have credit card records on Mr. Green's account that have him both places last night, at the right times."

"Do we have a time of death?" Burton asked.

"The temperature in the garage was cold enough to make determining her time of death difficult," Crown answered.

"What's your guess on how she died?"

"Preliminary examination suggests she died from a broken neck," Crown said. "But that doesn't mean she was murdered; she could have fallen."

"And I say Mr. Green killed her," Gibson said.

"Looks like these two theories are neck and neck," Trellis said. "Get it? Because she has a broken neck."

"Michael," Crown said to Trellis, peering at him over her glasses, "go get an autopsy kit. And suit up; you're going to assist me."

"Oh, man," Trellis said, his shoulders drooping as he went to get the tools.

"Wes," Crown said to Burton, "I've already checked the clothes and body for trace evidence; everything I found is bagged and labeled. If you could finish the photography, Michael and I will get started measuring and weighing the body and prepare for X-rays."

"You got it," Burton said and picked up the lab camera. He had to ask Gibson to move several times in order to take all the photos, and eventually the grumpy detective left the lab to go ask Mr. Green more questions.

"Finally," Burton said as the door closed behind Gibson. "I thought Mike was going to have to tell more jokes to get him to leave."

"I can tell some more anyway," Trellis said.

"No!" Burton and Crown said together. They finished with the weight, measurement, and X-rays. Crown placed the X-rays on a lighted wall panel.

"There are fractures here and here," Crown said, pointing at spots on the X-rays. "Mrs. Green did die from a broken neck, but that still doesn't prove murder. I don't see any external injuries; let's take a look inside the body and see if there is any internal damage."

"What is it we're looking for?" Trellis said, handing Crown a scalpel.

"If she received a blow to the head," said Crown, "it could have affected her balance, causing her to fall and break her neck." She made the Y-shaped incision on the body.

"Or she could have been drugged," Burton added.

"Possible," Crown said. She cut through the ribs and removed the breastplate to expose the heart and lungs, which she also removed. "We will run toxicology tests on the heart for any drug presence." Crown worked her way through the abdomen, removing and weighing each organ until she got to the stomach.

"The stomach feels full," Crown said, placing it on a separate, smaller examining table. She used the scalpel to open the stomach and remove its contents.

"Is that spaghetti and meatballs?" Trellis asked.

"Mostly," Crown said. "There is also some salad and bread." She pointed at something mushy. "That could be tapioca pudding, but I'm not certain."

"So Mr. Green's version of what happened checks out so far," said Trellis. "They did eat at the Primo Pasta Palace."

"That's true," Burton said. "But his story stops tasting good after that."

How did Burton know Green was lying?

Burton's File

After a meal, the stomach is usually empty within four to six hours. If Mrs. Green had gone dancing after the meal, her digestion would have worked even faster. Her full stomach indicates that she died within one or two hours of eating, which makes her husband a liar and, possibly, a murderer.

We later learned that Mr. Green killed his wife after dinner. He left her body at home and used his credit card at the Boogie Barn to make it look like he and his wife went dancing.

An Inferno Lie

Mike Trellis poked his head into the interview room and saw Gibson looming over some guy who looked like a lawyer and some other guy who was wearing a nice suit. Burton was yawning.

"Can I talk with you for a second?" Trellis asked the CSI. He was going to add "if you're not too busy," but Burton was already through the door, muttering something about a three-ring circus.

In the hallway, Trellis handed his arson investigation report to Burton and said, "I took plenty of photos and video. There really wasn't much damage to the house, no collapsing walls or falling floors. However, I was interested in the lightbulbs in the room where he kept his art collection."

Burton flipped to those photos and saw the lightbulbs. "They're intact," he said. "Not even distorted a little."

"Righto," Trellis said. "It usually takes about 900 degrees Fahrenheit, for around ten minutes or so, for lightbulbs to swell or distort. So this fire either didn't get hot enough or burn long enough to affect the bulbs."

"Good to know," Burton said and took the file with him back into the interview room.

"I'd like an explanation as to why my client is here," the lawyer said. The lawyer was William Hudson, and his client was Alan McFarland. McFarland wore a tailored three-piece suit and was carefully trimming his fingernails with a set of gold-plated clippers.

"Because Mr. McFarland had a house fire," Burton said, "and we have a few questions for him."

"Yeah," Detective Frank Gibson said, "and I have a few of my own for you, Mr. Lawyer. Just a 'what if?' kind of thing, you know? Like, what if I accidentally hit a suspect's head on the roof of my car while I was putting him in the back?"

"Well, that would —" Hudson said.

"Hold on," said Gibson. "I'm not done yet. What if, after that, he started to bleed all over my backseat, so I put him in the trunk? With my dirty laundry."

Hudson handed Gibson his business card. "You'll be needing this," he said.

Burton said, "Can we get back to Mr. McFarland now?"

"By all means, continue with other topics," said McFarland, who was now working on his left thumb. "This is a complete waste of time either way."

"I thought you'd want to make sure we got all the facts," said Burton. "From your insurance claim, it looks like you lost some art in the fire."

" 'Some art?' " McFarland said, an eyebrow cocked. "Listen, they have 'some art' in the bathrooms at the bus station. I lost priceless pieces of history. One of my porcelain bowls was worth more than the rest of my collection combined, and it was completely destroyed. But, like you said, my insurance claim will take care of it. So it looks like we're back to this being a waste of time."

"How do you file an insurance claim for something priceless?" Gibson said. "Do you just get all the money in the world and call it even?"

"No," McFarland said, "I take your annual salary and multiply by a hundred. And that's just for my shoes."

"Wow, you hear that, Burton?" Gibson said, his eyes big. "This guy's got a smarter mouth than you. Hey, McFarland, how'd you like to take a ride in the back of my car?"

"That's intent to cause bodily harm!" the lawyer said, standing up to get between his client and the detective.

"Not his body," said Gibson, stepping forward. "Just his head."

McFarland unfolded the little nail file from the clippers and held it in front of him. "Not without a fight!"

"All right, everybody calm down," said Burton. Gibson stepped back, but McFarland kept his nail file ready.

"I don't get it," Gibson said. "What's so special about this bowl? It's just a piece of clay, right?"

McFarland took a deep breath. "No, it's not. Porcelain is created through a long process of purification and requires an attention to detail you couldn't possibly understand. If one speck of dirt gets on the porcelain while it's being baked, it creates a stain that ruins the piece. And it sometimes has to bake for three days at more than 2,000 degrees. You don't even have the attention span to tie your shoes correctly."

Gibson looked down at his untied laces. "Naw, I keep them that way on purpose. Because it bothers people like you."

Burton said, "Untied shoes or not, the evidence will have no problem standing up in court."

"What evidence?" Hudson and McFarland said.

"The evidence that proves you removed your priceless bowl from the room before you set the fire."

How did Burton know?

Burton's File

Trellis pointed out that in a fire, lightbulbs begin to distort when they are exposed to temperatures around 900 degrees Fahrenheit for ten minutes. This is because the heat is causing the lightbulbs to melt.

*McFarland claimed that his priceless porcelain bowl was destroyed in the fire. Unfortunately for him, he also said that porcelain needs to bake for several hours at more than 2,000 degrees. The fact that the lightbulbs weren't affected by the fire indicates that the fire did not burn nearly hot enough or long enough to damage the porcelain bowl. McFarland wanted the bowl **and** the insurance money; now he'll get neither.*

An Uncivil Murder

Burton walked into the crime lab and saw Dr. Lauren Crown unzipping a body bag. Inside was a man dressed in a dark blue Union Army uniform from the Civil War, complete with a forward-scrunched forager hat and a bugle.

"What did you get?" Burton asked.

"Caucasian male, age forty-three. Cause of death: gunshot to the chest," said Crown.

"Finally, you can scratch that off your wish list," Burton said. Crown ignored him. Mike Trellis walked in reading a printout, and he didn't look up until he was next to the body bag. He looked inside the black material and almost dropped his papers.

"This body is perfectly preserved!" he said. "The Civil War ended in 1865; this man should be a skeleton by now!"

"Calm down, Michael," Crown said. "He was part of a Civil War reenactment group. They had an event over the weekend, and someone shot this man for real. The police department that handled the crime scene doesn't have the resources to investigate it, so they shipped him here."

"I've heard about those reenactments," Burton said. "They're pretty serious about getting things right. You can't even use slang that wasn't around during that period, let alone any equipment."

"The police report stated that may be the reason this man was shot," Crown said. "Witness accounts referred to him as having 'farby' items, things that wouldn't have been around in the 1860s. Farby actually means 'far be it from authentic.'"

"Like that?" Burton said, pointing at a cell phone clipped to the corpse's belt.

"What if the ring tone played 'Yankee Doodle Dandy'?" Trellis asked.

"That's the Revolutionary War," said Crown.

"Mike, grab that camera," Burton said. "It looks like the gunshot came from close range." He pointed to the burn mark surrounding the bullet hole in the man's coat. "The gun must have been within six inches to cause this charring."

"I see stippling in the fabric, too," said Trellis, leaning in for a close-up photo of the tiny particles of gunpowder that had been embedded in the coat when the gun fired. The fabric also had some dirt on it but was otherwise quite clean. "It's a very tight pattern, which also indicates the gun was close."

"Let's get this coat off the body to see what we can see," Burton said. The three of them got the body onto the examination table and managed to remove the thick, wool overcoat. Underneath that was a vest, and underneath that was a white polyester shirt.

"Man," Trellis said. "With all these layers, I'm surprised the bullet got through."

"It got through all right," said Burton, holding up the overcoat. There was another hole in the back. "In fact, it went all the way through him. Did the crime scene crew recover the bullet?"

Crown shook her head. "Everything they sent was in the body bag. They did confiscate all the guns that were involved in the incident, but they kept those at their station."

"How many guns?" Burton said.

"Fifty-seven muskets," said Crown. "All were fired that day, so we can't use your famous sniff test to see which one the murderer used."

"Hey, my nose is considered an expert witness in this county," Burton said. "Besides, I think we can use something else to find out which gun was used."

Trellis said, "I musket ready for this investigation. Get it? Musket? Must get . . ."

"I want you to leave," Burton said. "But I need your arson experience, so remind me to tell you to leave some other time."

"Arson?" Crown said. It almost sounded like she was confused, but Dr. Crown was never confused.

"Sort of," Burton said. "Mike, some arsonists use gunpowder, right?"

"Sure," Trellis said. "When they want things to go boom, not just burn. Gunpowder isn't the right term though. We call it smokeless powder."

"Who is 'we'?" Burton said.

"Those of us who know things you don't," said Trellis.

Burton shook his head. "Okay, so it's smokeless powder. Smokeless compared to what?"

"Black powder," Trellis said, "which was replaced by smokeless powder in the late 1800s. Apparently, the military commanders didn't like how the black powder produced so much smoke that they couldn't see the battlefield from up on their hills."

"What's the difference between the two?" Burton said.

Trellis eased back, taking his time in the spotlight. "Black powder is 75 percent potassium nitrate, 15 percent carbon, generally charcoal, and 10 percent sulfur. When it's ignited, there's smoke all over the place. And I mean *all* over the place. When someone fires a musket with black powder, it looks like the gun exploded. These days, black powder is only used for historical reenactments, like with our Civil War friend here."

"And the smokeless powder?" said Burton, though he wasn't very happy about having to ask his technician. "I imagine it's called that for a reason."

"Very observant of you, Wes," Trellis said, and even Dr. Crown rolled her eyes. "Smokeless powder produces much less smoke than black powder. Almost no smoke at all, really."

"So once we test the muskets," Burton said, "we'll be able to prove the owner is a killer and a hypocrite."

How will they find the murder weapon?

Burton's File

The blue coat on the murder victim had burn marks from the close-range gunshot, but no smoke residue. If he had been shot with a gun using black powder, the material would have been covered with soot from the smoky discharge. Instead, he was shot with a gun using smokeless powder, which had not yet been invented when the Civil War took place. All the other guns, in order to be accurate for the time period, would have black powder. The killer made a statement by killing the "farby" man with "farby" smokeless gunpowder. Now he'd better find a good lawyer to make his statements for him.

Appetite for Death

In the crime lab, Burton waited for the toxicology report for Grant Newton, the body lying on the stainless steel table. Mike Trellis saw Burton looking bored and offered him a broom.

"You could at least clean up while you wait," Trellis said.

"I wouldn't want to mess up your system," Burton said back.

"What system?" Trellis asked. "You sweep the dirt into a pile, then you put the pile in the garbage."

"Whoa, whoa," said Burton. "I'm already confused. You sweep the garbage into the dirt pile?"

"Fine," Trellis said and put the broom back. "If you want to stand there and not do anything while Dr. Crown and I break this case, that's just fine." Dr. Crown walked in and saw Trellis talking to Burton.

"Michael, we don't have any time for chitchat," Crown said. "There is too much work that needs to be done."

"Hey, but," Trellis said, his arms flapping, "I was telling *him* to get to work!"

"Perhaps we should lead by example," Crown said, peering at him over her glasses. Trellis looked at Burton, who smiled.

"That's a good idea," Burton said. "Maybe you could sweep while Dr. Crown and I break this case." Trellis stomped away, muttering under his breath. Burton walked over to Dr. Crown, who was standing over the body with the toxicology report in her hand.

"Anything conclusive?" Burton asked her.

"Mr. Newton had very low levels of sodium and potassium in his blood and tissues when he died," Crown said, looking at the report.

"Low enough to kill him?" Burton said.

"It's possible," said Crown. "It's like he'd been flushed clean."

"Do you think he was poisoned?" Burton said.

"There isn't anything on the tox report to suggest it," Crown said. "But it wouldn't have to be poison. Simply drinking massive amounts of water can cause fatally low levels of sodium and potassium in the body. It's called water intoxication. Do you suspect he was murdered?"

"Well," Burton said, "he had a house and lived alone, but there was enough food stockpiled in the place to keep a family well fed for the winter. Like he planned on being holed up there for weeks, maybe with a few friends."

"Perhaps he shops at one of those giant club stores," Crown suggested, making it sound like a crime. She only ate organic food that she grew at home.

"I thought of that," Burton said. "But it wasn't stuff that you can keep on the shelf, like canned goods, you know? He had fifteen pounds of oysters, ten cheesecakes, hundreds of hot dogs."

"That's enough," Crown blurted. Burton watched her

face turn from ivory to a sickly green; he'd never seen her get nauseous before.

"Mike! Get the camera!" he shouted.

"Don't you even think about it," Crown said, her jaw clenched. She swallowed once, then again, and had the illness under control. Burton was disappointed. Trellis stumbled over with the camera, ready to start clicking.

"What is it? Is it an alien?!"

"No," Burton said. "I thought Dr. Crown was going to vomit for a second."

"Oh, man!" Trellis said, even more disappointed than Burton.

"An alien?" Burton asked, cocking his head at Trellis.

"Forget I said anything," said Trellis.

"You should wear a shirt with that on the front," Burton said. "Let's go back to Newton's house. I need another look at the place. And I'm hungry." He looked back at Crown, who covered her mouth and pointed at the door.

At Newton's house, Burton again noticed all the food in the pantry, refrigerator, and freezer. "It's like he was planning something," he said. "Something that would make him stay inside for a long time."

"Or maybe this is our answer," Trellis said and handed a magazine to Burton. He looked at the cover: *Competitive Eater Monthly*.

"What in the world is this?" Burton said.

"Competitive eating," said Trellis. "That's why he has

all this food. They compete to see who can eat the most food in a certain amount of time. I guess Newton didn't have the stomach for it. The competition chewed him up and spit him out. Wow, that's two, right in a row. Get it?"

"No, I don't get it at all," Burton said. "There's no way this can be considered a sport."

"They train for it," said Trellis. "They drink gallons and gallons of water at a time to stretch out their stomachs. And apparently it's pretty competitive, because it looks like someone might have murdered Newton over it."

"Newton was killed, all right," Burton said. "And the killer escaped down the drain."

How did Newton die?

Burton's File

Dr. Crown mentioned water intoxication, which occurs when someone drinks enough water to severely dilute the sodium and potassium levels in their blood and tissues. Low levels of these substances can lead to kidney damage and eventual coma and death. Newton drank gallons of water at a time to stretch out his stomach for his competitive eating. He ended up drinking himself to death.

Falling for a Lie

Burton and Mike Trellis stood at the bottom of the 150-foot cliff, photographing the body of Rich Halpin.

"Do you think he felt sheer terror when he fell?" Trellis asked. "Get it? Because the cliff is sheer."

"That's a good one," Burton said.

"Really?" said Trellis.

"No," said Burton. "And according to Andy Konik, the guy he was hiking with, Halpin may already have been dead when he fell."

"Oh, yeah," Trellis said. "Have you ever heard of people getting robbed at gunpoint along a hiking trail?"

"Not recently," said Burton, "but it used to happen all the time. Back when cities only had one major road, thieves would wait in the woods alongside it. When a nice-looking carriage would roll past, they'd jump out and rob the people inside."

"Kind of like drive-thru crime," Trellis said.

"Hey down there!" Burton and Trellis both looked up to see Detective Erin Radley peering over the edge of the cliff. She said, "When you get a chance, come on up!"

Burton looked at Trellis and said, "This might be a good opportunity for you to listen to the witness's story. Get a feel for what happened."

"You just don't want to walk back up the cliff," said Trellis, still snapping photos.

"You should have been a detective," Burton said and started walking up the steep path to the left of the cliff face. When he arrived at the top, a little out of breath, Radley was talking with Andy Konik. He wore hiking boots and a backpack and looked pale despite his tan.

When Radley saw Burton, she patted Konik on the shoulder and said something to him, then walked over to Burton alone.

"He's pretty shaken up," Radley said. "Witnessing your friend die, that must be very hard. But it brings up an interesting point."

"Chapter 403 of your book?" Burton said.

"Funny," said Radley. "The point is, why would a killer leave a witness behind? He was already a thief, but you throw murder in and that's a whole different story. Maybe the killer got spooked and ran?"

"I don't like to deal with 'maybes,'" said Burton. "Maybe means more than one possibility, and that makes evidence tip over in court."

"So then, why murder?" Radley asked.

Burton said, "The best way to find out *why* is to know *how*." He and Radley walked over to Konik, who was staring over the cliff.

"Mr. Konik," Radley said, "This is Wes Burton. He's our lead crime scene investigator. I'd like you to tell him what happened."

"Okay," Konik said and took a drink from his water bottle. "Well, Rich and I were walking along the trail, and we stopped at the cliff to take a few pictures. Then this guy comes out of the woods behind us, pulls out a huge gun, and tells us to give him all our money. I gave him my wallet, but Rich didn't have anything except his camera, and he didn't want to give it to the guy, so the guy just shot him."

Burton walked toward the edge of the cliff, careful to avoid the area where the hikers had been attacked. There was a strong wind blowing toward the edge, and it made Burton a little nervous, like it could pick him up and toss him into the open air. "Where was Rich standing when he was shot?"

"Um, right about there," Konik said, pointing to a spot in the dirt that had boot impressions. "I was standing right next to him, about there." He pointed to a spot just to the right of the first. They were both about six feet from the drop-off.

"How did Rich end up at the bottom of the cliff?" Burton said.

"I told you, man," Konik said. "It was a really big gun. When Rich got shot, he flew back and over the cliff. It sounded like a cannon going off."

Burton walked over to Konik and inspected the front of his shirt and shorts. "I don't see anything here," he said to Radley. Konik took a small step backward.

"Hold still," Burton said. "Have you washed your hands since the shooting?"

"I rinsed them off, yeah," Konik said.

Burton said, "With this wind, there might not have been much anyway."

"Much what?" Konik said.

"Evidence that you shot your friend and threw him over the cliff," Burton said. "But I still think you'll take the fall."

How did Burton know?

Burton's File

Konik based his account of what happened on what he'd seen in the movies. No matter how big the gun is, a bullet will not cause a person to fly backward when shot. In addition, if Konik had been standing next to Rich when he was shot, the wind blowing toward the cliff would have deposited gunshot residue onto Konik's clothes. Since he was standing in front of Rich when he pulled the trigger, the wind carried the GSR away from him.

Intended Human Combustion

Burton and Mike Trellis stood in the dim living room looking down at what used to be Walter Pullman. From the charred remains, Burton could distinguish a skull, two hands, two feet, and a pile of ashes and internal organs where Pullman's torso used to be.

"This might be the best day of my life," Trellis said.

"Don't start," said Burton.

"I'm serious, boss," Trellis said, still staring at the remains. "This is my first case of spontaneous human combustion. I might be able to prove once and for all that it exists. I have a few theories of my own, and, if they turn out to be true, I could be famous."

Detective Gibson walked through the front door. "I have a theory that your head is empty," he said. "Let's go find a hammer and see how that one turns out."

"Just because you're here doesn't mean you get to share my fame," said Trellis.

"Mike, start taking photos," Burton said, handing him the camera. "Frank, what do we know about this guy so far?"

"Who, Trellis?" Gibson said. "Acts goofy, tells the worst jokes on the planet. And he has stupid hair."

"I already know that," Burton said. "I was asking about Walter Pullman." Trellis looked around for a mirror to see if his hair was okay.

"Walter Pullman," Gibson said, checking his notes. "Sixty-seven years old, lives alone, no close friends."

"That's it?" Burton said.

"That's it."

"Why do you even need a notebook?" Burton said.

"I plan on getting more information," said Gibson. "Besides, if it was spontaneous human combustion, the case is closed. Why should I get writer's cramp for no good reason?"

"See, Wes?" Trellis said. "Is it so unbelievable that something in the human body can cause it to suddenly burst into flames and turn the person into ashes?"

"Yes," Burton said.

"Come on, man," Gibson said. "This theory would make our jobs so much easier. When we find a body at a car wreck, maybe it was spontaneous human collision. And hey, when we get one with a bullet in the brain, let's write it up as spontaneous human gunshot-ation."

"You made that word up," Trellis said.

"What if we find a body in the stomach of a bear?" Burton asked the detective.

"Why, that would be spontaneous human consumption!" Gibson said.

"Fine," said Trellis. "But when I prove that it does exist, you two will not be in the movie of my life story."

"Pullman thinks a movie is funny," Gibson said, pointing at the skull on the floor, with its full upper and lower sets of teeth exposed. "See? He's got a big ol' grin on his face."

"Can you try to fill that notebook of yours with some more information?" Burton asked. Gibson shrugged and started poking around the house.

"Mike," said Burton, "You can't go into an investigation like this with an answer already in your head. If you do, you'll miss evidence. Like this — the internal organs are still intact, if a little crispy. If the fire had started inside the body, they would be destroyed."

"I didn't say it started in the center of his body," Trellis said. "The fire could have started just under the skin, in the hypodermis layer where there are fat deposits."

"And what was the source of ignition?" Burton said.

Trellis thought for a moment. "It could have been microwaves, a chemical reaction in his tissues, or a buildup of static electricity, to name a few possibilities."

"Maybe he passed gas too close to a candle," Gibson shouted from the bathroom, where he was rooting through the medicine cabinet. "There isn't anything in here to suggest he had any health problems, no heart pills or anything. Just some bad aftershave, a half-empty tube of denture adhesive, and Q-tips." Burton wondered what he could find out about Gibson by going through *his* medicine cabinet.

"No candle, no matches, no lighters," Trellis said. "Walter Pullman died from spontaneous human combustion, and I'm going to prove it."

"No, you're not," Burton said. "Because this isn't Walter Pullman."

How did he know?

Burton's File

Gibson said that Walter Pullman lived alone and had no close friends, indicating that all items in the residence would belong to Pullman. Gibson found denture adhesive in the medicine cabinet, which suggests that Pullman wore false teeth. The skull on the floor had a full set of teeth, indicating that Pullman, dentures and all, tried to fake his own death.

Not a Knife Way to Die

"I hate to think how long the guy would have been in there if his blood hadn't leaked into the storage unit next door," Jerry Perkins said. He was the owner of Safe Keepings Storage, a series of low metal buildings with garage-style doors.

"Probably until the spring thaw," Mike Trellis said, preparing his camera. "After that, he'd start to smell."

"The scavengers might find him before that," said Burton. "So it's good you called us. It's difficult to examine a crime scene when animals have carried parts of the victim away. You know, fingers, toes . . ."

"Don't forget the eyeballs," Trellis said. "I call them animal appetizers."

Perkins made a face. "You guys go on ahead. I'll hang back here."

"Works every time," Burton mumbled to Trellis as they walked away. They didn't like to work with gawkers standing around. Inside the nearly empty storage unit, Detective Frank Gibson stood, hands on hips.

"Man, I've been standing here freezing my ears off," he said. "I figured you geniuses got lost."

"We just followed the stench," said Burton.

"This body's fresh," Gibson said. "It doesn't stink yet."

"I wasn't referring to that body," Burton said.

"You know what your problem is, Burton?" said Gibson. "You're too smart for your own good."

"Something you'll never have to worry about," Burton said. "What do we know about Mr. Leaky here?" He pointed to the body in the back-left corner of the storage unit. The corpse lay in a large pool of blood.

"Single stab wound to the chest," Gibson said. "Guy's name is Adam Lewis. He rents this storage space for his antique-chair collection."

Burton and Trellis looked around at the complete lack of furniture.

"Are they invisible antique chairs?" Trellis asked, poking his toe around to test the area in front of him.

"We don't know where they are," Gibson said. "We talked to his wife, and she says the collection is worth a few hundred thousand dollars. She also said he had some gambling problems. My theory is that Lewis here had to sell his chairs to pay for his debts, and then killed himself out of guilt, shame, whatever. You'll find the knife there, next to his left hand."

"Is he left-handed?" Burton said, taking video of the scene while Trellis snapped photos.

"No idea," Gibson said. "I can ask his wife. You don't think it was suicide?"

"I don't think anything yet," said Burton, "because I don't know anything yet." He reached over the pool of blood and patted Lewis's pants pockets. "His wallet is in his left-front pocket, so that indicates left-handedness. But check with his wife just to make sure."

Gibson stepped outside to make the phone call, and Burton continued shooting video. He zoomed in on the knife lying next to Lewis's hand and narrated for the camera, "Thin, dagger-style knife, blade looks to be about six inches long and an inch wide; the blade is sharpened on both sides; wooden handle with a round guard between the handle and the blade."

Burton finished his moviemaking and turned the camera off. "Are you done with the photos?" he asked Trellis. "I'd like to take a look at the stab wound."

"All done," Trellis said. "If he was murdered, do you think the killer will get the chair? Get it? The electric chair. Lewis collected chairs."

"Seek help," Burton said. He slipped Tyvek booties from vest pocket 26 over his shoes and stepped next to the body, careful to not disturb the blood. He opened Lewis's shirt and exposed the stab wound, which was on the left side of the chest.

"Entrance wound is boat-shaped, with ragged damage at one end," Burton said.

"There's a bruise around it, too," Trellis said. "Looks rectangular."

"Good job," Burton said as he pulled a small ruler out of vest pocket 13. He placed it next to the wound. "About an inch and a half. Let's get some close-ups."

Trellis resumed taking photos and Gibson walked in. "The wife confirmed he's left-handed," he said. "So what do you think now?"

"I still don't think anything," Burton said. "I know he was murdered, and this isn't the knife that killed him."

How did Burton know?

Burton's File

The thin, dagger-style knife at the crime scene was sharpened on both sides and had a circular guard between the blade and the handle. Lewis's injury was boat-shaped and ragged at one end, indicating that the blade was thick, with a sharp edge on one side and serrations on the other. The serrated edge produced the ragged wound as the ridges passed through Lewis's skin.

When Lewis was stabbed, the knife entered with enough force to drive the blade all the way in, resulting in the guard between the blade and handle bruising his skin. The rectangular bruise indicates that the dagger, with its circular guard, was not the murder weapon.

Out with the Mold,
In with the Clue

"Bug, it's Saturday, don't you take any days off?" Burton asked as he and Mike Trellis got out of the crime scene truck. He'd parked in the street, in front of the mansion where Bug was working.

"What is day off?" Bug said through his black filter mask. "So much to clean up and only one Bug, you know?"

"Why don't you hire some help?" said Trellis.

"This work, it is not for everyone," Bug said. "Some peoples think they are too good to shovel rat poop or tear up carpet with blood and brains on it."

"How dare they?" Burton said.

"I know, I know," Bug said. "Like this job today. This woman, Ms. Walters, calls me and says she has black mold in house. Stachybotrys is actual name for mold, very dangerous. But I look through whole house and not find anything. Not even a water leak to cause the mold."

"Why does she think she has black mold?" Burton said.

"She has headaches," Bug said. "I'm thinking, who does not have headaches?"

"That's it? Just headaches?" said Burton.

"Well, that, and stomachaches like from flu, sore throat, numbing through body, hair loss . . . "

"All those, and you picked headaches to tell us first?" Burton said.

"Is first thing she told me," said Bug, holding his hands up.

"That's quite a list," Burton said. "So why did you call us instead of a doctor?"

"Woman says she thinks her ex-husband planted mold in house to kill her," Bug said. "She got house in divorce and thinks he wants revenge."

"That's a spore way to kill somebody," Trellis said. "Get it? Poor way, spore way?"

Bug thought about it. "No, Mikes, I do not . . . wait . . . Yes! Spores from mold! Bah ha ha! Mikes, you are best!"

"You want him, Bug?" Burton said. "He *loves* to shovel rat poop."

"That was only one time," Trellis said, his voice shaking. "And it was on a dare!"

"Is Ms. Walters inside?" Burton said, walking toward the front door.

"Yes, she was in kitchen when I walked out here," Bug said and followed Burton. Trellis collected the gear from the truck and mumbled about accepting dares from veterinary students.

"Ms. Walters, my name is Wes Burton, I'm with the crime lab."

"Hello," she said, popping two antacid tablets into her mouth. She crunched them down without water. "Did you arrest my ex-husband yet?"

"We'll probably need some more information before we

take that step," said Burton. "Why do you think he placed black mold in the house?"

"To get back at me for divorcing him," Walters said. "I got the house, the Hummer, the country club membership, and the other Hummer. All he got was a bill from my lawyer."

"And you suspect him of trying to harm you because of that?" Burton said.

"Harm?" said Walters, her eyebrow cocked. "He's trying to kill me. I did my research on black mold. Chronic exposure can cause cold and flu symptoms, fatigue, headaches, sore throat, hair loss, immune system suppression, memory loss, and severe brain damage."

"And a partridge in a pear tree," Trellis said, walking in with the gear. Everyone ignored him, except Bug, who laughed so hard he had to leave the room.

"Are you experiencing all of those symptoms, Ms. Walters?" Burton said.

"Not yet," she said. "But the ones I have are getting worse. Hair loss, nausea, extremely sore throat." She coughed to show them how sore it was.

"Why don't you move?" Trellis said.

"And give my ex-husband the satisfaction of chasing me out of this house?" she said. "Not a chance. Even though he thinks it has rats."

That brought Bug back into the room. "Rats?" he said. "I have not seen any rats. That is whole other cost to you."

"Well, I haven't seen any either," Walters said, "so I'm not paying you anything. Besides, my ex-husband put enough rat poison in this place to exterminate the species."

"That would be bad for business," Bug said. "Besides, I am much safer for getting rid of rats. Rat poisons have arsenic, is no good for you. It kills rats, yes, but it is poison to everyone."

The woman tried to figure out what Bug was talking about, then gave up. She turned to Burton. "So is there a specific crime for trying to kill someone with black mold?"

"No," Burton said. "But there is one for trying to kill someone with arsenic. It's called attempted murder."

How did Burton know?

Burton's File

Ms. Walters's symptoms could easily be mistaken for the effects of black mold, which typically grows best in a continually wet environment like a slow water leak inside a wall or ceiling. However, the fact that her ex-husband spread rat poison throughout the house, even though there were no rats, indicates that he tried to kill her using arsenic, which causes symptoms that include burning throat pain, nausea, hair loss, and numbing sensations.

The Baffling Blue Body

"I'm telling you," Mike Trellis said to Dr. Crown, "ulcers are caused by stress!"

"You're wrong," Crown said without looking up from the male body she and Trellis were observing on the examination table. The corpse was various shades of blue, making it look a bit like an alien. "And please calm down. You're spitting on the body."

"But I have an ulcer!" Trellis said. "I should know what it takes to get one."

"Why do you have an ulcer?" Burton said, walking into the exam room. "You don't have any stress."

"See?" Trellis said, his voice getting high.

Crown sighed. "Lifestyle factors such as stress and diet may have an impact on the severity of an ulcer, but the ulcer itself is caused by a bacterium named *Helicobacter pylori*. You can call it *H. pylori*, since you're already acquainted."

Trellis looked down at his stomach. "So I'm infected right now?"

"It's likely," Crown said. She finished drawing blood from the corpse and handed the sample to Trellis.

"Try not to die before you get that analyzed," Burton said to the technician. When Trellis slowly shuffled away, Burton watched Dr. Crown work. She didn't seem to mind, and he soon realized it was because she had forgotten he was there.

Burton tried to make small talk. "Did you see the news last night?"

"No," Crown said. "I don't own a television."

"Oh, that's right," said Burton. "How do you know when things are happening?"

"What things?" Crown said.

"You know, like weather, political scandals, celebrity weddings. Those things."

"The only item on that list that impacts me is weather," Crown said. "And I have windows. I even have doors, in case I want to step outside." She picked up a scalpel, and Burton thought it best to keep quiet for a while.

Eventually he said, "So this guy had an ulcer?"

"Correct," Crown said. "He had prescription bottles of amoxicillin and a proton pump inhibitor in his pocket."

"Proton pump inhibitor?" Burton said. "That sounds more like a murder weapon than a medicine."

Crown made a Y-incision on the body. "The inhibitors suppress stomach acid production, allowing the ulcer to heal faster."

"I guess it won't matter for this guy," Burton said. "When I saw the blue skin, my first guess was that he died from lack of oxygen. But there wasn't sign of struggle at the crime scene, just a spilled cup of tea on the floor. Usually, people who suffocate make quite a mess. His fiancée found the body and called 911, but I couldn't understand much of what she said."

"Because she's smarter than you?" Crown asked, pulling the skin away from her scalpel cuts.

"What? No," Burton said, then stopped. "Well, she could be, I guess. But I couldn't understand her because she's from Ecuador. Detective Radley is trying to find an interpreter now. So, she could know what happened but, even if she does, she might not tell us."

"Maybe he was just really sad," Trellis said, walking back with the toxicity report. "Get it? Because he's blue."

"Maybe telling horrible jokes causes ulcers," Burton said, taking the printout. He shook his head. "Nah, you'd have died years ago." While Burton read the toxicity report, Dr. Crown picked up her bone shears and started to cut through the ribs and collarbones so she could remove the breastplate.

"Curare?" Burton said, looking at the trace amounts the spectrometer had detected in the blood sample. "Isn't that a medicine used to stop the lungs during some operations?"

"It is," Crown said. "It's made from the bark of the *Strychnos toxifera* plant. Some Central and South American tribes use it to poison the tips of their arrows and darts."

"This guy got shot by a poison dart?" Trellis said.

"No, Michael," said Crown. "If you'll recall, you and I inspected the body, and there were no puncture wounds."

Burton said, "What if he ate it? Or drank it . . . or . . . rubbed up against it?"

"Curare is harmless when swallowed," Crown said. "It

has to be injected into the bloodstream or soft tissues. You mentioned that it's sometimes used during surgery, and that's true. It's also used as a muscle relaxant and an anticonvulsant."

"I'd better go talk to the fiancée," Burton said. "Maybe she tried to help him, but he just didn't have the stomach for it."

How did he die?

Burton's File

The victim's fiancée offered him curare-laced tea to relax him, hoping it would ease his stress and relieve the pain from his ulcer. Unfortunately, the victim absorbed the curare into his bloodstream through the ulcer in his stomach, causing rapid paralysis of the diaphragm and lungs. This led to suffocation and death.

The Crooked Carpet Deal

Burton and Mike Trellis entered the bank lobby and followed the shouting into one of the side offices. Detective Radley was already there, trying to calm down two men who looked ready to fight. She spotted the CSIs and a look of relief swept across her face.

"Mr. Barnes! Mr. Sanchez!" Radley said to the shouters. "Please sit back down and stop yelling. Our criminalists are here, and we can have this issue resolved shortly."

"Criminalists?" the man on the left cried. "The only criminal here is Sanchez! I can tell you that right now!" He pointed to the other man, who was nearly jumping out of his chair.

"The nerve!" Sanchez bellowed, and his chair almost tipped over.

"All right, take it easy," Burton said. "All this trouble over a rug?" Both Barnes and Sanchez turned on him, bug-eyed.

"A rug?" Sanchez said. "It's a sixteenth-century Persian carpet in perfect condition!"

"I've searched for years and haven't seen its equal!" said Barnes. "All the original yarns and weaving!"

"That's right!" added Sanchez.

"Okay, sorry, sorry," Burton said, holding his hands up. He turned to Radley, who looked like she wanted to knock Barnes's and Sanchez's heads together. "Can you get us up to speed without shouting at us?"

"I'll try," she said. "Mr. Sanchez had a Persian rug —"

"Carpet!" Sanchez corrected.

"Be quiet," Burton said.

"Mr. Sanchez had a Persian carpet," Radley continued. "He sold it to Mr. Barnes for fifty thousand dollars."

Trellis almost spit out his gum. "Fifty thousand dollars?" he said. "Does it fly?" Barnes and Sanchez looked at him, ready to start shouting, then saw Burton glaring at them. They stayed quiet.

"No," said Radley. "It does not fly. But like Mr. Sanchez said, it is an antique and worth a lot of money. So Mr. Barnes gives a money order to Mr. Sanchez for fifty thousand dollars, because a money order is almost the same as cash. It can't bounce like a check. But when Sanchez goes to cash it, the bank says the money order was originally for five thousand."

"So Barnes forged the check into fifty thousand?" Burton said.

"Yes!" Sanchez said.

"No!" said Barnes. "The money order isn't a forgery! The bank made a mistake, and now he wants the carpet back *and* the money!"

"He's trying to walk all over you, huh?" Trellis said to Barnes. "Get it? Because it's a carpet."

"You be quiet, too," Burton said to him, then turned back to Radley. "Is the carpet here?"

"Yes," she said. "The bank held on to the money order, so we have that, too. They're both in the manager's office."

"We'll be right back," Burton said, and he and Trellis headed for the manager's office. When they arrived, the manager took the rolled-up carpet out of her locked closet and retrieved the money order from a locked drawer. Burton examined the money order and didn't see any obvious tampering — no disturbed fibers in the paper from an eraser or indication of bleached ink.

"If this is a forgery," he said, "it's pretty good." He took his magnifying glass out of vest pocket 1 and held it over the money order.

"Don't set it on fire with the magnifying glass," Trellis said.

Burton didn't look up. "Just because it happened to you once," he said, "doesn't mean it'll happen to me."

Trellis looked at the bank manager and shrugged. "It wasn't my fault," he said. "The sun was too high that day." The manager nodded but obviously had no idea what he was talking about.

"I don't see any evidence of forgery so far, but we can check it out under UV. Before we do, I want to see what all the fuss is about. Mike, can you unroll that rug — I mean carpet?"

"It's okay," Trellis said. "You can call it a rug in front of me." He unrolled the carpet next to the manager's desk. "Man, it doesn't even have a cool picture on it, like of Elvis or Shaquille O'Neal."

The carpet did have a very nice design of tan, gold, deep reds, and blues, and it looked like a lot of work had gone into making it. There was a shape in the middle that looked like a flower vase, but Burton wasn't sure if that was what it was supposed to be.

"Do you need anything else?" the bank manager asked.

"Darkness," Burton said and closed the window blinds. "Please turn off the lights." That done, Burton snapped on his portable UV light from vest pocket 25. A bunch of lint showed up on the manager's dark-blue suit jacket, and she gasped.

"I just had this dry-cleaned!" she said.

"Lots of things show up in UV that we can't see in normal light," said Burton. "Maybe you should tell your dry cleaner to buy one. Now, let's have a look at the money order." He leaned in with the UV light and held it over the money order. He saw the forgeries immediately. "See here? Where 'Fifty Thousand' is written out? You can see the 've' where it used to read 'Five' instead of 'Fifty.' Even though Barnes erased the visible ink somehow, traces of it will still fluoresce under UV. And here, where the number is '50,000.' The zero after the five looks slightly different, because he couldn't use the exact ink from the original printing."

"So Barnes did forge the check," Trellis said. As Burton looked over at him standing next to the Persian carpet, he noticed that only half of the vase shape in the middle of the rug was visible in the UV light.

"He sure did," Burton said. "But Sanchez is lying, too. This whole deal should be swept under the rug."

How did Burton know?

Burton's File

Just as the two inks on the money order fluoresced differently, so did the two yarns in the Persian carpet, causing the vase shape to partially disappear. If the carpet had all its original yarns, as Barnes believed it did, the whole vase would have appeared under the UV light. The two yarns indicate that at some point it had been repaired, which makes Sanchez a fraud.

The Fatal Phone Booth

Burton and Mike Trellis parked the crime lab truck near the end of the block and walked toward Detective Gibson, who was standing next to a phone booth.

"Here, take this," Burton said and handed Trellis his CRIME SCENE — DO NOT CROSS | CRIME SEEN? STICK AROUND tape from vest pocket 2. "I don't want anyone stumbling into that phone booth and tainting evidence. Make sure you get the tape far out enough to preserve any broken glass on the cement." The glass hadn't shattered, but Burton could see some small shards sparkling on the sidewalk. Gibson saw them approaching and started to grin.

"This doesn't look good," Trellis said.

Gibson said, "Hey, I have a good one for you: How many CSIs does it take to process a double shooting?"

"How many?" Trellis asked before Burton could warn him not to bite.

"None," Gibson said. "I already solved it."

"That's not very funny," Trellis said.

"What do you mean you solved it?" Burton asked. Sometimes, Gibson's definition of "solved" meant he'd arrested everyone involved.

"I know these two guys. They have a long history of disliking each other. The guy inside the phone booth is Tom Watts, and the one outside is Nathan Lipton," Gibson said.

"They shot each other, and both the shooters are dead, so what's the point of investigating?"

"Now *that's* funny," said Burton and handed the camera to Trellis. "Any eyewitnesses?"

"None so far," Gibson said, his tone implying that he didn't think it mattered.

Burton said, "We still need to know what happened, and with both shooters deceased, there isn't anyone who can tell us."

"Wrong!" Gibson said, the grin reappearing. "I checked the last number dialed from this phone and called it. The lady on the other end said she was talking to Watts, then she heard some yelling, then two loud bangs. Gunshots, I'm guessing."

"Brilliant," Burton said. "So what happened?"

"I just told you," said Gibson. "Watts was talking on the phone, and Lipton walked up and they started yelling. Then they shot each other."

"Who fired first?" Burton asked.

"Who cares?" Gibson said.

"Family members, lawyers, insurance companies, media, and us, just to name a few," Burton said.

"Bah," said Gibson, waving it all away. He walked over to his car, leaving Burton and Trellis to process the scene.

Burton looked at the two bodies. "They were both shot in the chest, which means they were face-to-face. If one of them was shot in the back, that could tell us who fired first."

"I wonder if Watts called his shot before he fired," Trellis said. "Get it? Because he was on the phone."

"I like Gibson's joke better," Burton said as he stepped around the outside of the phone booth for a closer look at the glass. The bullet holes were about chest high and a foot apart.

Burton pointed to the hole on his right, which was closest to the street. "We'll refer to this one as Hole A, and the one closer to the sidewalk as Hole B. Both bullets went through the same pane of glass, but they didn't shatter it. Let's get some close-up photos of the holes from both sides."

Together, the bullet holes looked like two sloppy spiderwebs. Both had cracks running away from them like spokes on a wheel, and the spokes from each hole ran into each other at several locations, making intersections of cracks.

Burton said, "The cracks from Hole A end when they hit the cracks from Hole B. The Hole B cracks continue on after those intersections."

Trellis took photos of the key locations, then stepped into the phone booth, careful not to disturb Lipton's body. "I can see that Hole A is cone-shaped from this side," he said, taking a close-up photo of the hole, which from inside the booth was like looking through the top side of a funnel. "So Lipton, outside the phone booth, fired the bullet that made Hole A?"

"Correct," Burton said. "The bullet passing through the glass knocked out a cone-shaped plug as it exited the other

58

side. I see the same thing on Hole B from out here, so we know Watts fired the bullet that made Hole B from inside the booth."

Gibson approached and said, "So, did you guys figure out that these two didn't actually shoot each other and that they were in fact abducted by aliens 400 years ago and beamed back down to confuse us?" Trellis looked up at the sky suspiciously.

"Not quite," Burton said. "But we did find out that Watts fired first. Any other story is just phony."

How did Burton and Trellis know?

Burton's File

When a projectile, or in this case, a bullet, passes through glass without shattering it, it leaves a clean hole on the entrance side. It also knocks out a cone-shaped plug on the exit side. That indicates that Hole A was from a bullet fired by Lipton from outside the phone booth, and Hole B was from a bullet fired by Watts from inside.

The cracks from Hole A end when they meet a crack from Hole B, indicating that the cracks from Hole B were there first. If Hole A was made first, its cracks would continue past those of Hole B.

The Greenhouse Grave

Burton and Ed the border collie pulled up to the house in the crime scene truck. It was a large house, and it had a FOR SALE sign in the front yard with a SOLD! sticker on it. A woman was waiting for them in the driveway, her arms folded in front of her.

"That must be Mrs. Sweeney," Burton said to Ed. She glanced at him and swished her tail. She knew it was time to go to work, and she was getting excited. In addition to her search-and-rescue qualifications, she had been certified as a cadaver dog just a few weeks earlier. Most dogs sniffed for dead things as a hobby; now Ed got to do it on the job. Burton parked the truck and let Ed out on her leash, then walked over to the woman in the driveway.

"Mrs. Sweeney?" he asked, his hand out.

"What kind of real estate company sells a house with a dead body buried in the greenhouse?" she demanded. Burton withdrew his hand.

"I don't think it's on many checklists," he said. "Lead paint, asbestos, termites, those are all there. But corpses in the greenhouse? Not really a popular item for a real estate inspection."

"Well, it ought to be," Mrs. Sweeney said. "What if it's the last person who bought the house, and the real estate people just killed them and put the house back on the market?"

"Then we are in extreme danger," Burton said, and Ed

growled in agreement. "Maybe we should locate the body before we start identifying it."

"Follow me," Mrs. Sweeney said, stomping around to the side of the house. There was a police officer standing outside the greenhouse in the backyard, and Burton stopped to talk with him.

"Did you see anything in there?" Burton asked Officer Gates, who was trying to find something in his pockets that Ed would like.

"I didn't see anything, no," Officer Gates said. "But it smells pretty awful inside. Something's been rotting away for a while." He produced a small baggie of baby carrots and held them up for Burton's approval.

"She might like one," Burton said, knowing that Ed would gladly snarf the whole bag. Officer Gates presented a carrot, and Ed offered her paw in return. He shook it and gave her the vegetable, which she crunched and swallowed in two seconds.

"I wish my kids would eat their veggies like that," Officer Gates said.

"I wish Ed would take out the garbage and mow the lawn," said Burton. Ed gave him a look that seemed to say *I would, but the neighbors might stare.* Mrs. Sweeney was standing next to the greenhouse door tapping her foot and looking at Burton. He wondered if she knew that tapping her foot in grass didn't make any sound.

"Do we know who lived here last?" Burton asked.

"Dr. Timothy Donnard," Officer Gates said, checking

his notes. "He used to be a professor at the university. Botany or something."

"He's a doctor of plants?" said Burton.

"According to the real estate agent who sold the house," said Officer Gates. "She said he moved to Sumatra."

"That's in Indonesia," Burton said.

"Right," said Officer Gates. "We're trying to locate him now, but, hey, it's Sumatra."

"Okay, Mrs. Sweeney, let's take a look," Burton said, bringing Ed up to the greenhouse. "Now, it could be a dead animal that someone buried and not a dead person."

"We thought of that, too," Officer Gates said, pulling out his flashlight. "But why would someone bury an animal inside the greenhouse?"

"Maybe it was a pet," Burton said. "Or maybe something just crawled in here and died."

"Maybe," Officer Gates said, and Burton noticed that he and Mrs. Sweeney were both looking at him. It seemed like they were waiting for something. Then the smell hit him, and he realized what they were waiting for.

"Whoa!" Burton said. The stench was overpowering and smelled like rotting meat. Ed wagged her tail.

"Still think it's a dead animal?" Mrs. Sweeney asked, her eyebrow cocked.

"Maybe a water buffalo," Burton said as he entered the greenhouse. "Wait here, please," he said to Officer Gates and Mrs. Sweeney.

"No problem," Mrs. Sweeney said.

Ed went to work, sniffing the ground and sorting out the odors she didn't need. Burton marveled at how she could follow the scent of decomposing flesh when, to him, it filled the greenhouse and seemed to come from everywhere. The glass building was filled with colorful exotic plants that he had never seen before, and he was glad that Mike Trellis hadn't come on this call. Trellis lived in terror of giant, man-eating Venus flytraps, and this place would not help his fear.

When she couldn't find a trail, Ed switched to air scenting, her nose twitching as she followed the rotten flesh smell to its source. Burton walked behind her and pulled a filter mask out of vest pocket 15. It helped a little, but the scent was still in his nose.

Suddenly Ed stopped and sat down, her way of telling him that she had located the corpse. Burton rewarded her with a few pats and a treat from vest pocket 27. He surveyed the ground in front of her but didn't see any disturbed soil that might indicate a grave. In fact, the dirt was covered with a blanket of vines that would have certainly been disrupted if a hole had been dug.

"Are you sure this is the right spot?" Burton asked Ed.

Her look said, *Who do you think you're dealing with?*

"Okay," Burton mumbled. "But a body that smells this fresh would have been buried recently, and those vines have been there a while. See, even that giant flower is undisturbed." Flies buzzed around the orange-red flower, which was at least two feet across, then flew into a bowl at its center. Burton took a closer look at the blossom, then gave Ed another treat.

63

Outside, Mrs. Sweeney and Officer Gates were waiting for the news.

"Is it Dr. Donnard?" Mrs. Sweeney asked. "It is, isn't it? Oh, I knew those real estate people couldn't be trusted!"

"No, it isn't Dr. Donnard," Burton said. "In fact, the corpse is quite alive."

Where is the dead body?

Burton's File

There is no dead body, but it's no surprise that Mrs. Sweeney thought there was a decaying corpse in her greenhouse. The rafflesia flower, also known as the "stinking corpse lily," is a rare, endangered plant found in Indonesia. It uses the smell of rotting meat to attract insects, which then carry its pollen to other rafflesia flowers.

The Killer's Tall Tale

Burton and Trellis walked toward the front door of the one-story house. Detective Erin Radley was waiting for them on the overgrown concrete that led to the entrance.

"Morning, guys," Radley said.

"Mmm," said Burton.

"The boss hasn't had any coffee yet," Trellis said, "so I'll interpret. He said, 'And a good morning to you as well, Detective. You're looking quite nice today.'"

"Why, thank you, Wes," Radley said, looking at Trellis. "Wait a minute." She stepped next to the technician and squinted at his head. "Are you getting taller?"

"Nah," Trellis said. "It's these new boots. They make me about an inch taller. And they give me more sole. Get it? Sole, soul?"

"Mmm," Burton said again.

"Do you feel that extra height equals extra authority?" Radley said. The extra inch in Trellis's boots made him almost as tall as Radley, who stood 6' 1".

"Uh-oh," said Burton. He could almost see her taking out her mental notepad, collecting information for her book.

"Um, no, I just like the boots," Trellis said.

"I see," said Radley, nodding.

"Is that a bad answer?" Trellis asked, getting worried.

"I guess that depends," Radley said.

"I'm taking these boots back," said Trellis.

"Can we solve this crime first?" Burton said.

"I don't feel qualified to answer that," Trellis said. "These boots have ruined everything."

Radley smiled. Mike was always a good warm-up for interviewing suspects. "I'll give you the details before we go inside," she said. "The victim is Ellen Underwood, killed sometime last night. I have two suspects, Jim Danielson and Larry Saunders, who were both seen here with Underwood last night."

"Seen by whom?" Burton said.

"Each other," Radley said, cocking an eyebrow. "Danielson says he left first, so Saunders must have killed her. Saunders says he was the first one to leave and that Danielson must have done it. I know what you're going to say. Something about eyewitness accounts having glasses, not shoes, so they won't stand up in court."

"That's not bad," Burton said.

"Both guys are down at the station right now," said Radley. "I don't see either one of them changing his story, so we're going to need some hard evidence to get the killer to confess."

"Let's go see if the killer was nice enough to leave any evidence," Burton said and walked inside. "Mike, start taking video of the house, I'll handle the photos. We don't know how big the crime scene is yet, so let's get everything on film." They worked from room to room, eventually arriving at the doorway to the kitchen. Ellen Underwood's body was on the floor.

"Looks like she was killed in here," Burton said, still standing outside the doorway. He indicated the blood spatter on the floor and cupboards. "She wasn't murdered somewhere else and moved to this room."

"I tried to get the killer to trip up," Radley said, "and mention something about the kitchen without me asking. But neither one did, so I had to come out and ask if they had been in this room. They both say they never went in the kitchen."

"I like the kitchen," Trellis said, "that's usually where the cookies are." He stepped into the doorway to get video of the room, his head almost touching the top of the door frame.

"Freeze!" Burton said, and Trellis dropped to the floor. Burton and Radley both looked down at him. "Man," Burton said, "that's the worst freeze I have ever seen."

"I thought you saw someone else in the house," Trellis said, still facedown on the floor. "I just wanted to clear your field of fire, in case you had to shoot."

"Always thinking," Burton said. He stepped over the technician.

"What do you see?" said Radley.

"I see a brown hair," said Burton, taking several photos of the strand, which was stuck to the wood trim above the doorway. "It's about an inch long and probably stuck to the wood with hair gel or wax." He took an evidence bag out of vest pocket 9 and a set of tweezers out of 24, plucked the hair off the frame, and sealed it in the bag.

"Both Danielson and Saunders have short brown hair," Radley said. "And I don't think we have enough probable cause to get DNA samples from either of them for comparison."

"How tall are they?" Burton said.

Radley thought about it. "Danielson is probably around five-nine or so. Saunders is a little taller than me, so I'll put him at six-two."

"That's enough DNA information for me," Burton said. "Tell Saunders we can prove he was in the room where Underwood was killed."

How did Burton know?

Burton's File

When Trellis walked into the kitchen doorway, his head almost touched the top of the frame. With his new boots, he stood about 6' 1", which makes the door frame a little higher than that. Saunders, at 6' 2", is the only suspect who would have been tall enough to brush his head against the frame and leave a hair sample behind.

The Lethal Landlord

"I already told the detective there what happened," Bobby Henderson said, pointing at Detective Gibson. Gibson was standing in the brightly lit dining room of a very dirty house. There were holes in the walls, stains on the carpet, and burns on the furniture.

The detective was looking at the large, shattered, sliding glass door and, just inside the house, the shotgun lying on the table. Outside the now-glassless door, on the wooden deck, Mike Trellis was photographing the dead body of Sammy Kent. There was a pistol lying next to Kent's right hand.

"I'm sure you won't mind repeating your story for me," Burton said. "Besides, it's almost midnight. When it's this late, Detective Gibson needs to hear things a few times before he remembers them."

"Um, okay, I'll tell you," Henderson said, looking nervous, like maybe the shooting wasn't done. "Sammy and I own — well, he doesn't anymore, I guess. We used to own this house, which we rented to college kids. They trashed the place every year, and the costs to keep it up to code were taking all our profits. So I wanted to rent to families only, since they would take better care of the property."

"You should meet my neighbors," Gibson said. "They have seven kids, which I consider to be a family, and their place looks like a toxic dump."

"Maybe they keep it that way to cover the smell of your cologne," Burton suggested. "Mr. Henderson, please continue."

"All right," Henderson said. "So we disagreed about what to do with the property. Sammy wanted to keep the college kids, because we can charge $400 per tenant. If we have four tenants, it's $1,600, if we have six tenants, it's $2,400."

"I can do the math," Gibson said.

"Really?" Burton asked.

"But with a family," Henderson continued, getting into landlord mode, "we can't charge that way, because for some reason, parents don't want to pay the same amount for the kids as they do for themselves. Something about them not taking up as much space."

"How selfish of them," Burton said. "So you wanted to charge less money but have cleaner tenants, and Sammy wanted to charge more money and keep the college kids."

"Right," Henderson said. "But his way costs more in repairs, so my way is better."

"So you shot him," Burton said.

"Whoa!" Henderson said, his hands up in front of him. "No, no, no. Well, yes. I did shoot him, but not because we disagreed. It was self-defense. I got here at about 8 o'clock to look at the damage the last tenants did and change the locks, and he called me and said he was going to make me see things his way."

"That sounds like it could be a threat," Burton said.

"That's what I thought," Henderson said. "So I got my

shotgun out of my trunk, just in case. Around 9:30 or so, I was right about where I'm standing now, looking at the holes in the drywall, when I saw Sammy standing out on the deck pointing a gun at me. So I shot at him through the glass."

"Did he fire his gun?" Burton asked.

"No," said Henderson. "At least I don't think so, it happened pretty fast. But he was going to."

"Mike," Burton called. "Was that pistol fired recently?" Outside on the deck, Trellis carefully knelt next to the gun and sniffed the barrel.

"Not within the last few hours, for sure," Trellis said. "But it's hard to tell with Gibson's cologne overpowering my senses. My nose won't stop running."

"I'll run that nose right off your face if you don't pipe down," Gibson said.

"Have you changed anything in this room since the incident? Turned any lights on or off, moved any chairs?" Burton asked Henderson.

"No, I haven't touched anything," Henderson said.

"Why do you think Sammy came around to this door?" Burton asked Henderson.

"Like I said, I was changing the locks," Henderson said. "Sammy didn't have the new keys yet. But I think he was trying to sneak up on me."

Burton nodded. "I'll be right back," he said and stepped out onto the deck. "How's it going out here?" he asked Trellis.

"The yard is in worse shape than the house," Trellis

said. "There must be at least five old charcoal grills out there, if you can see them through the insane grass, and an empty aquarium for some reason. And it looks like the college kids liked to party in the dark." The technician pointed to the light fixtures on either side of the sliding glass door. "They're both broken and, from the rust I saw, they've been that way for a while."

"Did you get photos?" Burton asked.

"I got all the shots we need," said Trellis. "Well, not all the shots. Henderson got one. Get it? Because he fired the shotgun."

Burton looked at the body and said, "You're lucky you're dead and didn't have to hear that." He walked back inside.

"Are we about finished?" Henderson asked. "I've got a lot of cleaning to do."

"Not really," Burton said. "But our jail cells are already pretty clean."

Why is Henderson guilty?

Burton's File

With no lights on the deck and the dining-room lights blazing, the sliding glass door would have looked like a mirror to Henderson; he would not have been able to see Sammy pointing a gun at him. Henderson changed the locks and waited for Sammy in the darkened dining room, then shot him when he approached the sliding glass door.

72

The Piled-High Lie

Burton and Mike Trellis walked carefully around the body of Larry Van Patton, which was sprawled across the upstairs bedroom floor. He'd been killed with several blows to the head with the table leg that was lying near his body.

"I wonder how much of this mess is from the burglary," Trellis said, "and how much is from Van Patton being a slob." The room was a wreck, with clothes, dresser drawers, and pieces of lamp scattered everywhere. Trellis made sure to get a photo of everything from various angles.

"I'm not seeing much dust on these surfaces," Burton said as he examined a nightstand for fingerprints. "So I would wager that Van Patton was a pretty tidy person."

"Man, the thief sure tore the place up," Trellis said. "Wouldn't that be nice? Van Patton comes home to find his house trashed, he goes upstairs to see what's been stolen, and whoops — the burglar is still here! Then he gets killed."

"If that's the way it happened," Burton said.

"We have the burglar in custody," Trellis said. "What's his name? Wait, Herbert Knox, that's it. He confessed to the robbery and the murder. Although he says that he killed Van Patton in self-defense."

"You're going to trust a burglar's version of what happened instead of the evidence?" Burton said. "Remember: the defendant sits down in court, the evidence stands up."

"Right," Trellis said and got back to work. "I have a

fingerprint on this drawer, but it's too close to the carpet. I don't think I can get it." The dresser drawer was at the bottom of a pile of clothes and an open suitcase that looked like it had been pulled from under the bed.

"Go ahead and move the stuff if you have to," said Burton. "We have all the photos and video in case we need to see how it was positioned." Trellis took the drawer out of the room so he could lift the print without disturbing anything else. Burton looked at the carpet where the drawer used to be and saw spots of blood, either spatter from Van Patton's head or cast-off from the table leg as Knox swung it. He was taking photos of the stains when his cell phone buzzed. He took it out of vest pocket 18 and saw that the caller was Detective Gibson.

"Morons Anonymous, how can we help you?" Burton said into the phone.

"Huh? This is Detective Frank Gibson."

"You're the worst anonymous moron in the world," said Burton.

"Listen, do you know what CSI stands for?" Gibson asked.

"Cool Studs Incorporated?" Burton guessed. Trellis stuck his head in the room and gave him a thumbs-up. He wanted to have business cards with that phrase.

"No," Gibson said. "Civilians that Shouldn't be Investigating."

"Where did the *t* and *b* come from?" Burton said.

"I added them in," said Gibson.

"You're not supposed to do that."

"Do you want to know why I called?" Gibson asked, getting upset.

"I hope it wasn't to tell me that joke," said Burton. "Even Mike would have stayed away from that one." Trellis peered in again, looking confused.

"I just got the rap sheet for Knox," Gibson said. "He has a history of breaking and entering, along with some connections to organized crime."

"Has he changed his story at all?" Burton asked.

"No, he admits he was robbing the place," Gibson said. "But when Van Patton came home, he didn't give Knox a chance to escape. So Knox killed him and took off. He's still saying it was self-defense."

"So Knox left right after he killed Van Patton?" Burton asked.

"Yeah," Gibson said. "In self-defense, of course."

"Tell him he should have stolen a better lie," Burton said.

How did Burton know?

Burton's File

If Knox had left immediately after killing Van Patton, there would not have been anything on top of the bloodstain on the carpet. The drawer, clothes, and suitcase piled on top of the stain verify that Knox killed Van Patton before he burglarized the room. The robbery could be a cover-up for the intentional murder of Van Patton.

The Rotten Rider

Burton and Mike Trellis stood over the crime lab examination table, looking down at the blue-tinged corpse of George Semark while Dr. Crown examined it. Semark was dressed in a long-sleeved shirt and long pants and still had a bicycle helmet strapped to his head.

"How long do you think he's been dead?" Trellis asked.

"Since he was outside, it's difficult to determine exact time of death," Crown said. "The moisture, temperature, and other variables can all affect decomposition. My estimation is that he died approximately forty-eight hours ago, possibly three days. I'll check the potassium levels in the vitreous humor; that should give us a good indication."

Burton and Trellis watched her extract a sample of the fluid from Semark's eyeball.

It took a large amount of self-control for Trellis not to cover his own eyes. "Why do they call it vitreous humor?" he asked. "It's not funny at all. It should be called vitreous disturb."

"You call some of the things you say 'jokes,' and they aren't funny, either," Burton said.

"Yeah, but they don't make you nauseous," said Trellis.

"Wanna bet?" Burton replied.

"Gentlemen, please," Crown interrupted. "Tell me what you know about this case."

Burton took his notepad from vest pocket 3 and flipped

to the most recent page. "Semark was found by park rangers about five miles from his campsite. He and his friend Hans Berger were on a mountain biking trip; Detective Radley is with Berger in the interview room right now. He says that three nights ago, he woke up and found Semark in a state of delirium, acting crazy. Then Semark ran off into the woods. Berger chased after him but got lost. He finally found his way back to the campsite the next day, but no sign of Semark. He waited another day for him to show up, then rode his bike to the ranger station. They found Semark's body this morning with the help of search dogs."

"Were you and Ed there?" Crown asked. Even though she didn't enjoy talking with most people, Dr. Crown could spend hours chatting with Ed the border collie. Burton didn't know what they talked about, but it made him nervous.

"No, we weren't on the call," Burton said, clearly disappointed. "Ed and I did a nighttime tracking exercise last night, and we were worn out."

"Dog-tired, huh?" Trellis said. He grinned.

"I think I'm nauseated," said Burton. "Anyway, the whole story doesn't sound right to me. Radley had some good questions: Why did Semark run into the woods when he had his bike right there? Why did Berger wait a day before he went to the ranger station? Was he getting rid of evidence? He's the only one who was there, so he could say anything."

"Maybe determining Semark's cause of death will answer some of those for you," Crown said, and began preparing her tools. "Michael, please prepare the body for autopsy."

"Hey, are you dead?" Trellis said to the corpse. When he got no response, he looked at Dr. Crown. "The body is prepared." Crown looked at him, and after a few seconds of laughing at his own joke, Trellis began cutting the shirt off Semark's body. He started by slicing up the shirtsleeves. He didn't get very far before he stopped. "Um, Dr. Crown? You might be a bit off with your time of death. This guy has some serious rot going on."

Crown and Burton moved in to take a look.

"Interesting," Crown said. "The face and hands show almost no decay, but this area around the inside of his left elbow suggests he's been dead longer. The rotten flesh is much more advanced than the exposed parts of his body. It's like something was eating away at his tissues."

"Hold on one second," Burton said and walked over to the crime lab phone. He called the interview room, and Radley picked up on the third ring.

"Radley," she said.

"Burton here. Did Berger mention if Semark complained about arm pain before he started acting weird?"

"He did," Radley said. "Apparently, Semark had a bike accident the day before he took off. His front tire hit a pile of old logs, and he went over the handlebars, right into the decaying wood. Berger said Semark seemed fine until his arm started to hurt a few hours later. Why, does he have a broken arm?"

"We don't know about that yet, but —"

"I wouldn't be surprised, you know," Radley said, getting

on a roll. "This Berger guy is pretty smooth. I don't know what his motivation for lying is yet, but I'll find out. I'm using a new technique that will be in my book, I call it 'The Trapdoor.' See, what I do is, I ask a series of questions that —"

"I'm sorry, I have to go, Erin. Thanks for the info."

Back at the examination table, Crown was starting to look for more signs of advanced decay on Semark's body. If he had been dead longer than three days, she knew Berger's story was a lie.

"Don't bother, Doctor," Burton said. "I think we already have our killer."

"Berger confessed?" Trellis asked.

"No," Burton said. "He didn't have anything to do with it. Our suspect is hiding in a pile of logs."

How did Semark die?

Burton's File

When Semark wrecked his bike and ended up in a pile of old logs, he had an encounter with the brown recluse spider, which later bit him on the inside of the elbow. After a few hours, the spider's venom began to kill the tissue surrounding the bite, which explains the intense arm pain Semark experienced and the advanced decay in that area. The bite would not have been fatal if he had received medical treatment, but fever and delirium caused Semark to run into the woods. There, the venom continued to work and eventually killed him.

The Search for the Search Dog

"Hey, buddy! Get away from my dog!"

"What are you talking about? This is my dog!"

Burton could tell the owners of the voices were not happy. He and Ed the border collie were in the forest at the state park with a dozen other search-and-rescue teams. They were running practice drills, and there was a lot of barking and tail-wagging.

"Is there a problem here?" Burton said, walking over to the two shouting men. They had a bloodhound sitting between them, and he looked relieved to see something that wasn't yelling.

"Who are you?" the man on the left said, his tone still upset. He had a name tag that read GARY. The man on the right's tag said OSCAR, and a third man, labeled RALPH, stood off to the side.

"I'm Wes Burton. I'm with the police department crime lab." All three men looked at him then.

"Really?" Gary and Oscar and said together. Ralph stayed quiet.

"Really," Burton said. "You two seem to be disagreeing about something."

"Yeah," Gary said. "I say he's trying to steal my dog, and he says he isn't."

"Untrue!" Oscar yelled. "He's trying to steal *my* dog!"

Burton said, "Is this the dog?" He pointed to the blood-hound, who licked his chops and drooled.

"If you mean is this my dog," Gary said, "then yes, it is."

"What is his name?" Burton asked.

"Furley," Oscar said.

"Jeffrey T. Jupiter," Gary said at the same time. The bloodhound wagged his tail.

"See?" Oscar said. "He knows his name is Furley!"

"He was wagging about Jeffrey T. Jupiter!" Gary hollered.

"All right, calm down," Burton said. "Calling a dog's name doesn't prove identification. Some dogs respond differently when their name is called, and sometimes they don't respond at all." He gave Ed a sideways look, but she pretended not to notice. "Let's start with what happened. Gary, you first."

"Okay," Gary said, taking a deep breath. "We were on the last drill, doing a ground-scent search for Ralph here, who was pretending to be lost." Ralph nodded.

Gary continued, "Jeffrey T. Jupiter was off-leash and far enough ahead that I couldn't see him. When he found Ralph, he gave his signal, which is a bark. I caught up to Jeffrey T. Jupiter and told him, good job, then this guy runs up and tells me to get away from his dog! Can you believe the nerve?"

"Amazing," Burton said. "Your turn, Oscar."

Oscar said, "I let Furley off his leash after he sampled Ralph's scent article. He likes to mash his nose against the samples and get a really good whiff."

"Amateur," Gary said.

"Be quiet," Burton said and gestured for Oscar to go on.

"When I let Furley go, he took off like a shot into the woods and was, of course, the first one to find Ralph. When I caught up, Gary was patting Furley and telling him good job. I told him to get away from my dog, and he calls me a liar!"

"I did not!" Gary said. "But I am now! This is Jeffrey T. Jupiter!"

"Furley!" Oscar insisted.

"Enough," said Burton. "Why isn't the dog wearing any identification or a search-and-rescue vest?" As if to rub it in, Ed scratched her ear, causing her ID tags and the bells on her vest to jingle.

"Furley outgrew his last one," Oscar said, "and I didn't get a chance to pick up a new one yet."

Gary said, "Jeffrey T. Jupiter's vest is at the seamstress. He's getting his name embroidered on it."

"Aw, that's nice," Ralph said. Burton looked at him. Ralph shrugged.

"What were you using for the scent article?" Burton asked.

"Ralph's glasses case," Oscar said and held up a sealed transparent bag. The blue plastic glasses case was inside.

"I'm gonna need that back," Ralph said.

"Not just yet," said Burton as he took the bag from Oscar. He pulled a piece of paper out of vest pocket 3 and softly pressed it against the bloodhound's nose for less than a second. The bloodhound wagged his tail and drooled. "These will tell us which one of you has to start searching for your search dog."

How will Burton find out?

Burton's File

Just like a person's fingerprint, a dog's nose is unique to that dog. When Furley mashed his nose against the glasses case, he left a nose print on the surface. If that print matches the sample on the paper, it means that everyone will start searching for Jeffrey T. Jupiter. If not, Furley is the one that's lost.

The Severed Singer

"Well, it's a one-car garage, but where is the car?" Burton wondered. He was talking to himself, but Detective Radley answered.

"The deceased's car is parked along the street," she said. "Apparently he put it there when he and the band practiced in here. They were called the Screeching Statues. As you can see from their instruments, they don't play classical music."

The bass guitar, resting on top of an amplifier along the wall on their left, was shaped like a large battle-axe. Along the back wall, the drums looked like large, black witches' cauldrons, and the electric guitar leaning against the right wall looked a lot like a skeleton.

"Cool," Mike Trellis said, and he meant it. "And this guy was the lead singer?" he asked, looking at the body lying in a large pool of blood near the middle of the garage floor.

"That's right," said Radley. "The rest of the band says it was an accident, but I wonder if the slit throat is someone's way of telling him they didn't like his screeching."

"Yeah, maybe they cut him from the band," Trellis said. "Get it? Because his throat is cut."

"Go wait in the truck," Burton said.

"Really?" said Trellis. He sounded almost hopeful. With the amount of blood in the garage, Trellis knew there was a lot of work to do.

"No, get to work," Burton said, then turned to Radley. "So the band was rehearsing, and the lead singer cut his own throat by accident?"

"That's what they're saying," said Radley. "I talked to the drummer, the bass player, and the guitar player, and they all said the same thing: the singer liked to swing his head back and forth with his eyes closed when he performed, and he somehow managed to catch his throat on the microphone stand and rip it open."

"Maybe it couldn't *stand* to listen to him anymore," Trellis said. "Get it?"

Radley ignored him. "The rest of the band didn't notice it at first, because their show involves them acting like statues while they play, staring straight ahead and only moving their arms. The drummer isn't very good at it, though, so he was looking at his drums. Once they realized what was happening, they tried to help him, but he'd already lost too much blood."

Burton leaned toward the body for a closer look. "It looks like both the internal and external left carotid arteries are severed," he said. "He would probably have lost consciousness within a minute, and death would occur soon after that from blood loss." Burton looked at the microphone stand lying on the floor. The stand had spikes sticking out of it, and several of them near the top had blood on them.

"So the singer was standing here with the guitarist standing next to him like a statue," Burton said, pointing near the body. "The singer's throat gets cut by the microphone stand,

85

and he probably leaned to his left after it happened, because the arterial spurts of blood hit the ceiling and trail down the wall to his left." Burton pointed out the blood trail with his finger, following it from above the singer and over to the wall where the skeleton guitar sat. The blood on the wall was a series of near-solid lines, with a few droplets scattered around.

"Could the blood on the wall be spatter?" Radley asked. "Maybe from some kind of weapon?"

"Nope," Burton said. "Think of the carotid artery as a hose. If you connect the hose to a pump like the heart, you get spurts of water that trail off at the end as the pressure drops off. So if you sprayed the ceiling with the hose at an angle, the initial spurt would hit the ceiling; as the pressure decreased it would trail down the wall."

"I knew that," Trellis said without taking his face away from the camera he was holding.

"I count six blood spurts along the ceiling and wall," Burton said, "so the singer stood here and bled for six beats of his heart before he moved or collapsed. Average resting heart rate for an adult is sixty to one hundred beats per minute, and the singer looks like he was in good shape, so we'll put him around sixty. Maybe higher, since he certainly wasn't resting."

"So he stood there for less than six seconds before he fell," Radley said.

"That's right," Burton said. "Plenty of time for the guitar player to play something sad while his victim died."

How did Burton know?

86

Burton's File

The singer's arterial blood spurts shot across the ceiling and down the wall to his left, where the guitarist should have been standing during the statue routine. If the guitarist had been there, the blood would have hit him instead of the wall, creating a void in the blood pattern. Instead, the guitarist was in front of the singer, pushing the spiked microphone stand into his neck while the singer swung his head back and forth with his eyes closed.

The Truth Is Within Arm's Reach

Burton and Mike Trellis tramped through the fallen leaves and found Detective Gibson standing next to a man wearing camouflage pants, shirt, boots, gloves, and a bright orange hat and vest.

Gibson saw the CSIs approaching and mumbled something to the hunter, who cracked a small smile. Burton and Trellis looked at each other and rolled their eyes. When they were close enough, Gibson said to the hunter, "This is Wes Burton and Mike Trellis. They're crime scene investigators, but that doesn't mean a crime went down, so don't freak out." The hunter nodded at Burton and Trellis, not sure if he should be glad they were there. "We're going to step over there and talk for a bit, so you stay right here."

The hunter nodded again and looked for a place to sit. There wasn't one, so he put his hands in his pockets. Gibson started walking away, and Burton and Trellis walked with him.

"Okay, guys," Gibson said. "That's Fred Sanders. We belong to the same gun club and hunt together every now and then. Not today, though. Today, Fred accidentally shot Wayne Jenkins in the chest. The EMTs are working on him over there, but he hasn't regained consciousness since the shooting."

"Did Sanders say it was an accident?" Burton asked. "Or are you assuming?"

"He said so," Gibson replied, his voice firm. "And I'm more than assuming. I've known these guys for ten years. They're good friends. And expert shots, I might add. They don't shoot anything they don't mean to."

"So you're saying Sanders meant to shoot Jenkins?" said Burton.

"No!" Gibson said.

Trellis leaned in to Burton and whispered loudly, "That's what it sounded like to me."

"Me, too," Burton loud-whispered back.

"Both you guys can go jump off a cliff," Gibson snarled. "You know, Jenkins probably wouldn't even be mad at Sanders. He'd be mad about missing the shooting tournament at the gun club next week, for sure. He's been the winner for the past six years. That's what good shots these guys are; Sanders has come in a close second for five of those six years; you don't get that good by shooting things accidentally."

"Does that mean we should go home?" Burton asked. "Case closed due to victim not being mad?"

"What if he dies?" Trellis said. "Case closed due to victim not being alive?"

"I like that," said Burton. "That would close a lot of our cases, and we wouldn't have to do anything."

"All right!" Gibson interrupted. "Do what you have

to do. The EMTs are getting ready to take Jenkins to the hospital."

"What did Sanders say happened?" asked Burton. Gibson didn't need to refer to his notes when he answered.

"The two of them were standing next to a fallen tree," Gibson said. "Jenkins went to step over the log, lost his balance, and grabbed for something to stop his fall. He happened to grab the barrel of Sanders's gun and pulled it toward him. Sanders's finger slipped into the trigger guard, and the rifle fired into Jenkins's chest."

Burton and Trellis walked toward the ambulance where the unconscious Jenkins was being attended to, and Burton pointed to the pile of camouflage clothes on the ground.

"That must be his jacket," he said to Trellis. "Check the entrance hole in the fabric. I'll take a look at Jenkins." They split up, and Burton leaned in over the EMTs working on the wounded hunter.

"How's it look?" he asked.

"Through-and-through, near the heart," one of the EMTs said. "It doesn't look good." The bullet had entered the chest, gone through Jenkins's left lung, and exited his back. Burton looked closely at the entrance wound. It was a small black circle with a little blue halo around it. There was a small amount of black smudging around the hole as well, but no unburned gunpowder had been embedded in the skin.

"No stippling around the wound," Burton noted to himself, and took a tape measure out of vest pocket 13. "Pardon me for one second," he said as he crouched next to Jenkins.

He measured the length of Jenkins's arms from the armpit to the tips of his fingers and jotted the results in his notebook: Left arm: 23 inches; Right arm: 23.25 inches. The EMTs continued to work but gave him strange looks. When he was done, he walked over to Trellis, who was taking photos of the hunting jacket.

"What did you find?" Burton asked.

"The jacket's clean," Trellis said. "No burn around the bullet hole, no powder, no soot." Burton nodded and waved to Gibson. The detective walked over, but Burton almost didn't want to tell him the news. Almost.

"We need to place Sanders under arrest," he said. "He might be a straight shooter, but he's lying to us about the shooting."

How did Burton know?

Burton's File

Sanders said that Jenkins grabbed his rifle barrel and pulled it toward him. If that were the case, the gun would have been within Jenkins's reach, which was about 23 inches. If the barrel was within 23 inches of Jenkins, the gunshot would have embedded traces of unburned gunpowder, called stippling, in the jacket. With no stippling, the gun was more than 23 inches away from Jenkins, indicating that Sanders was lying about the incident.

The Truth Stings

"I never lived in the dorms when I was in college," Mike Trellis said as he and Burton walked toward the large brick campus building. It was 10:45 P.M., but there were plenty of students still walking around.

"Why not?" asked Burton.

"Because they wouldn't let me set up my chemistry set. Something about possible massive explosions," said Trellis.

"And I thought this was a free country," Burton said as they entered the college dorm. A uniformed officer met them at the elevator and told them to go to the third floor. When the doors opened again, Detective Frank Gibson was standing in the hallway.

"It's about time!" Gibson said when he spotted the CSIs.

"Is he being sarcastic?" Trellis said to Burton.

"I can't tell," Burton said. "Usually, he'd rather see a tornado than us."

"Come on, you guys," Gibson said, waving them over toward a closed dorm room door. "Before they escape!"

"Before who escapes?" Burton said.

"The scorpions!" Gibson said. Burton knew Gibson didn't like snakes, and assumed that scorpions were also on his list of things to avoid at all costs. This would be fun.

"There's one right there," Burton said. He pointed to a piece of gum stuck to the floor next to Gibson's shoe.

"Gaa!" Gibson said and high-stepped away.

"Oh, nope, sorry," said Burton. "Just gum."

"Knock it off," Gibson said. "This girl over here got stung by a scorpion. Her name's Shelly, and she keeps them as pets, if you can believe that." He pointed toward a young woman sitting in the hallway. Two EMTs were huddled over her, taking blood pressure readings and applying a tourniquet to her leg.

"Hold on," Trellis said. "They wouldn't let me have test tubes and a Bunsen burner, and this kid gets to have scorpions? Who's in charge around here?"

"She's not supposed to have them," Gibson said. "That's how they got out. The dorm was doing a room inspection, and Shelly hid the scorpions under her bed. When the inspection was over, she went to put them back in their cage, but they were gone. She starts looking around for them, and one shot out from under her desk and attacked her."

"Scorpions don't attack people," Burton said. "Just like almost every animal in the world, they don't go after humans unless they're provoked or scared. I'm going to talk to Shelly and see what we're dealing with here."

"Ask her if we should set up a sting operation," Trellis said. "Get it? A sting operation? Because she got stung."

"When you go in there, use your face to check under the desk," Gibson said to Trellis.

Burton walked down the hall and knelt next to Shelly while the EMTs continued to work on her. He introduced himself and said, "How are you feeling?"

"My foot really hurts," Shelly said. "Like it's on fire."

Burton looked at the swollen and discolored foot, and saw a small blister near her little toe.

Burton said, "Any numbness or tingling along your leg?"

"No," Shelly said.

"What color are the scorpions?" said Burton.

"Kinda reddish," Shelly said.

"Okay," Burton said. "You should be better in about twelve hours or so. The sting isn't fatal, but it'll be sore for a while."

"How do you know that?" one of the EMTs asked.

"I do search-and-rescue work with my border collie," Burton said. "Sometimes, the search dogs and their handlers disturb snakes, spiders, scorpions, and so on. So I read up on the symptoms and effects of their venom."

"And I'm going to be okay?" Shelly asked.

"This is probably something you should have found out before you welcomed scorpions into your room," Burton said, "but the sting from a red scorpion isn't lethal. Black scorpions are more dangerous, and the really toxic ones are pale yellow with slender claws."

"Hold on," one of the EMTs said and started taking notes.

"The deadly stings don't leave much damage at the site," Burton continued, "so your swelling, discoloration, and the blister there indicate that it was a non-lethal dose."

"Thank you," Shelly said. "Can you please not hurt Klaus and Rudolf?"

"Who?" Burton said.

"My scorpions," she said. "Klaus didn't mean to sting me. He was scared because he and Rudolf were out of their home. And the detective said that he was going to find them with the bottom of his shoe."

"Don't worry about him," Burton said. "He won't even go in the room, I guarantee it. When was the last time Klaus and Rudolf molted?"

Shelly thought about it. "They shed their outer layer about a month ago. Why?"

Burton took his handheld ultraviolet light out of vest pocket 25. "I'd like to give them a glowing review of their performance this evening."

How will Burton find the scorpions?

Burton's File

All species of scorpion give off a green fluorescence when exposed to UV light. The glow is caused by a substance they excrete from their outer layer of skin. However, if a scorpion recently molted and its outer skin hasn't hardened yet, it will not fluoresce under black light. In this case, Klaus and Rudolf glowed green when the UV light hit their skin.

The Vomiting Van Man

"I think I'm going to throw up again," Charles Sutter said. He was sitting in the interview room with Detective Erin Radley and CSI Wes Burton, who slid the trash can over to him. It had a new bag in it since Sutter had already used the last one. Apparently he'd had a lot to eat.

"I still can't use the bathroom?" Sutter asked, wiping his sweaty forehead.

"There could be evidence," Burton said.

"That's nasty," Sutter said and heaved into the can again.

"Do you always vomit when you're nervous?" Radley asked. She'd never seen a suspect do this before, and she wondered if it was worth putting in her book about why criminals committed crimes.

"Who's nervous?" said Sutter. He was hugging the trash can against his chest. Radley handed him the box of tissues. He looked at it and set it back on the table.

"If you're not nervous," she asked, "why are you vomiting so much?"

"I'm in shock," Sutter said.

"Shock?" Burton asked, clearly suspicious. "You robbed four ATMs, then led police on a three-hour car chase in your big yellow van with the tinted windows. Which isn't a very good getaway car, by the way; not easy to hide." Sutter nodded. "Anyway," Burton continued. "How can you be in shock? You were driving the van, you knew what was going on. Nothing should be shocking to you."

"Shock is a strange thing," Sutter said, as if that explained everything. Burton noted that Sutter was nauseated, pale, and clammy, some symptoms of shock, but he wasn't experiencing extreme body temperatures, and when Radley checked his heart rate it had been normal. But he had a point; shock was tricky.

"Are you done with the trash can for now?" Burton asked. Sutter waited a moment, then handed it over. "I'll be back in a few minutes," Burton said to Radley.

"We'll be here," she said. As Burton left the room, he heard her say, "So, Mr. Sutter, why rob ATMs? Don't you like interacting with people?"

Burton walked into the lab, where Dr. Crown and Mike Trellis were running tests on the contents of trash bag 1.

"Did Chuck give it up?" Trellis asked. "Get it? Because his name is Charlie, and he's puking. Upchuck."

"He's confessing," Burton said. "And for that joke, you get to carry the vomit from now on." He handed the trash can to Trellis, who peered inside and recoiled instantly.

"Did you find anything relevant in the first batch?" Burton asked Dr. Crown.

"Before I answer your question," she said, "I have one of my own. During the police pursuit, did the officers ever lose sight of Mr. Sutter?"

"We can review the tapes from the chase cars," Burton said, "but I was listening to the radio during the pursuit, and they did lose him for about a block at one point."

"Bingo!" Trellis said, and held up a hand for Dr. Crown to high-five. She looked at it, her hands never leaving her lab coat pockets. Trellis let his hand down slowly.

"Bingo what?" Burton asked.

"We found traces of diphenhydramine and chlorotheophylline in Mr. Sutter's vomit," Crown said. "Two drugs that combine to form dimenhydrinate, which is used to treat motion sickness."

"Sutter is carsick?" Burton said. "That makes more sense than him being in shock."

"Who said he was in shock?" Crown asked.

"He did," Burton answered.

"He's lying."

"Okay. So we know he's carsick," Burton said. "Does that deserve a 'bingo'?"

"Let me explain something to you," said Crown.

"Oh, man, this is going to be good," Trellis said as he pulled a lab stool over.

"When you get carsick, or have motion sickness of any kind," Crown began, "it's a result of conflicting messages in your brain. Say you're riding in a car. If you look at something inside the car, such as a book or the person next to you, your eyes tell you that you're sitting still."

"Okay," Burton said, nodding.

"However," Crown continued, "the body's sense of balance is controlled by the inner ear, which knows that you are in motion, because the car is moving. So this conflict between what the eyes see and what the inner ear knows is what causes nausea."

"Got it," Burton said. "So what does that —"

"I'm not finished," Crown said.

"Oh, man, I knew this would be good," said Trellis.

"If you're driving the car," said Crown, "you look at the road, street signs, passing objects. You anticipate the results when you hit the gas and brakes. In other words, you don't have a conflict, because the eyes and inner ear agree that you are in motion."

Burton thought about it for a moment. Suddenly his head snapped up and his eyes grew wide. "Good work, you guys!" he yelled. He headed for the interview room at a near run. He opened the door and found Radley taking notes while Sutter was babbling something about never making the lacrosse team. He stopped talking when Burton put his hands on the table and leaned in close.

"Who was really driving that van," Burton said, "and where did he go after you let him out?"

How did Burton know?

Burton's File

If Sutter had been driving the van as he claimed, he would not have been carsick. As Dr. Crown explained, the driver has no conflict between the eyes and the inner ear. Before the police pursuit lost sight of the van for a block, another person was driving while Sutter got carsick despite taking his medicine.

Where There's a Will, There's a Crime

"Nice place," Mike Trellis said as he and Burton walked toward the brick mansion with the perfect lawn and spotless driveway. "Too bad the owner's dead."

"The previous owner is dead," Burton corrected. "We're here to see who the next owner will be." He spotted Detective Radley at the front door, waiting for them. "Hello, Detective," he said. "Has anyone else died during the reading of the last will and testament?"

"Not yet," Radley said. "But I'd say there's a fifty-fifty chance. Graham Wellington, the owner, was ninety-three when he passed away. Now his whole family is here waiting to see who's going to get what in his will. It's fascinating to see how some people mourn. Maybe that could be my next book: *Reactions to Death*."

Trellis said, "You'll have to have a couple of chapters titled 'Eww!' and 'Gross!' Because that's how most people react."

"Or they almost faint," Burton said, looking at Trellis.

"That was one time!" Trellis said, his voice getting higher with each word. "I mean, come on! There's a dead guy alone in a basement, surrounded by clown dolls. What would you do?"

"I wouldn't almost faint," said Burton.

"Not to mention run outside and call my mom," Radley added.

"Well, I guess you two are just superheroes then, aren't you?" Trellis said, stomping inside and muttering about how there better not be any clown dolls in the house. Burton walked with Radley through the huge foyer and into a dining room that echoed when they talked.

"So some of the family members are complaining about the will?" Burton asked.

"That's right," said Radley. "The two sons are accusing the three daughters of forging Mr. Wellington's signature on a false will. The sons think the estate lawyer might be in on it, too, since he also works for the daughters."

"Why do they think the will is a fake?" said Burton.

"Because they only get a million dollars apiece," Radley said.

"Boo hoo," said Trellis.

"Exactly," said Radley, "but when you consider that the daughters are getting ten million apiece, and ownership of the estate and the company that their father owned, things do get a little suspicious."

"Let's take a look at the document," Burton said, and he and Trellis followed Radley into a large family room, which just happened to be filled with family. As they passed through, Burton could see the two sons and their families on one side of the room. They looked happy to see the team of investigators, and one man even gave Burton a thumbs-up.

102

Across several couches, tables, and rugs, he saw the three daughters with their families. They were not as happy to see Burton and Trellis, and they glared and whispered to one another.

Burton smiled and nodded to everyone on his way through the family room and into a large den with dark wood paneling and built-in bookcases.

"This is Mr. McNally," Radley said, introducing the man standing next to a huge oak desk. "He's the estate lawyer executing the last will and testament."

"What did the will do to warrant the death penalty?" Trellis asked. "Get it? Because he's executing it." McNally looked horrified.

Burton rolled his eyes. "Mr. McNally, I'd like to examine the will, please."

"Of course," McNally said, but he didn't sound happy about it. He brought the document out of one of the desk drawers and set it in front of Burton.

"Do you have any other samples of Mr. Wellington's signature for comparison?" Burton asked.

"Mr. Wellington was very careful about his signature," McNally said, "just in case a situation like this ever arose. He didn't leave any signatures in the house, so if someone managed to steal a company checkbook, they wouldn't be able to forge his signature."

"That was smart thinking," Burton said, "but if we don't have a signature to compare the one on the will to, we can't verify that the will is authentic."

"I can verify it!" McNally sputtered. "I was there when he signed it!"

"Mr. McNally," Radley said. "We're trying to find the truth here. If you're telling the truth, you should help us."

"Very well," McNally said as he reached into his brief-case. "Here is the document establishing me as the executor of the will. Mr. Wellington signed it three weeks before he passed away."

Burton took the document and held it so Wellington's signature was next to the one on the will. He pulled his magnifying glass out of vest pocket 1.

"The pen used to sign the will was a little larger," he said, noting how the ink was fatter than on the executor document.

"What does that mean?" McNally said.

"Nothing," Burton said, "unless Mr. Wellington used the same pen to sign everything."

"No," said McNally, "he used whatever pen was closest."

Burton examined the signatures again. "I don't see any hesitations or pen lifts," he said. If the signature had been faked, the forger may have checked his or her work before it was done, lifting the pen off the paper and restarting several times. He took a small flashlight out of vest pocket 8 and pointed it at the signatures to get a better look.

He started with the light directly above the documents, then brought it down so it shone across the signatures at an angle, creating shadows wherever there was a dip or rise in the paper. The signature on the will was indented into the paper, and the ink filled the indentations completely. The signature on the executor's document also had an indentation, but the ink did not fill the depression completely.

"Mike," Burton said, "can you take a picture of this? No flash, please." Trellis walked over with the camera and took several photos from directly above the signatures.

"What is it?" Radley asked.

"It looks like Mr. Wellington's signature on the will," Burton said, "but it's actually Mr. McNally's signature on his arrest warrant."

How did Burton know?

Burton's File

McNally put his executor's document, which had the only example of Wellington's signature in the house, underneath the phony will and traced the signature. The pen he used was slightly larger than the one Wellington used when he signed the executor's document, which caused the indentation on the executor's document to be larger than the ink.

Where Wolf?

"Just to clarify," Burton said, "the man who bit you was dressed up like a werewolf?" It was Halloween, and he and Mike Trellis were wearing costumes of their own. Burton was dressed up as Sherlock Holmes, complete with deerstalker hat and curved pipe, and Trellis wore a homemade "CSI Wes Burton" costume. Detective Erin Radley wore her usual black leather jacket.

"Not dressed up!" Randy Lankford said. "He's a real werewolf! And now I'm going to be a werewolf!"

"Let me see that bite mark again," Burton said. "Mike, can you get some close-up shots of this?" Lankford held out his right arm for Burton. The oval bruise on the inside edge of his forearm was a deep purple. The mark was almost perfect, but there was a gap on each side, where the corners of the mouth would be during the bite.

"Well, now, let me just get my camera out of vest pocket 307," Trellis said, rooting through the oversized fisherman's vest he was wearing. "Ah, here it is. No, wait, that's my lunch from two years ago. Why do I have so many pockets?"

Burton shook his head. "When you do find your camera, let me know. Mr. Lankford, did you wash the bite?"

"Of course I did," Lankford said. "Human bites are filthy. Why wouldn't I wash it?"

"We could swab it for DNA," said Burton. "You may have washed it all away, but we can try anyway."

"Is there a test for werewolf DNA?" Lankford said. "I betI'mtransformingalready.Ismynosegrowing?MaybeIought to just chop the whole arm off."

"I wouldn't do that just yet," Radley said. "Do you know the man who bit you?"

"He's my neighbor," said Lankford. "I moved here three months ago, and at first I thought he was just a weirdo. But lately he's been running around his yard at night, howling at the moon and digging holes. I like to sit outside and listen to the crickets and other night sounds, and every time he acts like a wolf, he ruins it. Then I saw him tonight, all furry and insane. He came running up to me, and I could tell he wanted blood!" Lankford expected a response, but Burton and Radley just waited for him to go on. Trellis, still pretending to be Burton, continued to look in his vest pockets.

Lankford continued. "So he runs up, and I held my arm up in front of me to protect my face, and he bit my arm."

"And this happened tonight?" Burton said.

"About an hour ago, right before I called 911," Lankford said. "And by the way, tell that phone operator I don't appreciate her laughing when I told her I'd been bitten by a werewolf."

"I'll pass that on," Burton said.

"Hey, there he is!" Lankford said, pointing into the yard next door. A shadowy figure lumbered across the grass to the garbage can and dropped some trash into it.

"Mr. Lankford," Radley said, "please stay here with CSI Trellis while we go speak with your neighbor."

"CSI Trellis?" Trellis said, still acting as Burton. "He's a funny guy. I really look up to him and admire his crime-solving skills. Now where is that family of squirrels I keep in vest pocket 79?" Lankford rubbed his arm and looked confused.

Burton

and Radley, flashlights in hand, headed for the neighbor's yard, where the shadowy figure was sniffing around the garbage can.

"Biting is a pretty personal assault," Radley said. "It's very primitive, and obviously you have to come in close contact with your victim. It takes up a whole chapter in my book. Saliva can contain as many as a hundred million organisms per milliliter, with almost two hundred different species. You'd be amazed what kinds of infection you can get from a human bite: hepatitis B, hepatitis C, tuberculosis, and tetanus, just to name a few."

"I notice 'werewolf' wasn't on that list," Burton said.

"I've learned to never rule out anything in this job," said Radley. "But I'm pretty confident Lankford won't be turning into a werewolf anytime soon." They were getting close to the garbage can, and Radley raised her voice. "Excuse me, sir, I'm Detective Radley, this is CSI Burton. We'd like to ask you a few questions."

"Ruff-huff!" the furry man said, jumping back from them. Radley stopped where she was, planted her feet, and put her hand on her gun. Burton also stopped but only had his Sherlock Holmes pipe.

Radley said, "Sir! Stop right there, stand up straight, and face me!" She and Burton had their flashlight beams on him, and it was obvious that he was not a werewolf. Just very hairy.

"Whoa!" the man said. "Okay, easy, I thought you were trick-or-treaters. Please don't shoot me."

Radley took her hand off her gun but didn't relax. "We're investigating a complaint made by your neighbor. He says you bit him."

The hairy man smiled, showing a row of very white teeth with one of the top-front ones missing. "He said that? Man, what a liar. I didn't bite him. He's just upset about me rehearsing for tonight."

"Rehearsing for what?" Burton said.

"I love Halloween," the hairy man said. "Every year I get dressed up like the Wolfman and scare the neighborhood kids. The guy next door just moved in a few months ago, so he didn't know about it. I went over there tonight to see if he wanted to team up, like he could be Frankenstein or the Mummy, but he freaked out and ran inside."

"And called us," Radley said.

"Yeah, I guess," said the hairy man. "So it's my word against his?"

"No," Burton said. "It's his word against the evidence. And the evidence has more teeth."

How did Burton know Lankford was lying?

Burton's File

A bruise is blood that has leaked under the skin. As the blood changes color, so does the bruise, and the change follows a predictable pattern. A new bruise will be reddish, since the blood is fresh. It typically takes 1 to 2 days to darken to the deep purple of the bruise on Lankford's arm, indicating that he did not receive the bite within the last few hours as he claimed.

The shape of the bite indicates that it wasn't even the hairy neighbor who did the biting. If he was the chomper, the missing upper-front tooth would not have left a near-perfect bite mark.

A Certain Type of Bomber

I WILL BOMB PAPA'S PIZZA. REVENGE WILL BE MINE.

"Who would want to blow up Papa's Pizza?" Mike Trellis said. "They have great dipping sauces." He and Burton were in the crime lab, looking at the bomber's type-written note. It was sealed inside a plastic bag to prevent any contamination or damage.

"I don't think pizza sauce has ever stopped someone from committing a crime," Burton said.

"Not just pizza sauce," Trellis said. "Dill sauce, garlic butter, ranch . . . they're all quite delicious."

"Are you done?" said Burton. "Can we get back to the note?"

"Yes, but I really want some sauce right now," said Trellis. "Just so you're aware."

"Noted," said Burton. "Okay, let's start over." He read aloud, "I will bomb Papa's Pizza. Revenge will be mine."

"Revenge for what?" Trellis said.

"I spoke with Papa, the owner," Burton said. "And —"

"His name's really Papa?" said Trellis.

Burton took a breath. "No, his name is Francis. Papa is his nickname."

"Good choice," Trellis said. "Because that would be weird, naming a kid Papa."

Burton continued. "I spoke with Papa, and he said there

are two people he thinks might want to close his restaurant. One is a former business partner who thinks Papa ripped him off, and the other is a former employee who got hurt while he was working and had to quit. Gibson is looking into the two suspects right now."

"I'll bet he is," Trellis said. "He probably ripped them in half and is staring at their guts, trying to find the truth."

"Probably not," Burton said.

"Do you get it? Because you said he was looking into them."

From right behind Trellis, Gibson boomed, "And you're next."

Trellis jumped two feet straight up in the air and farted. He landed and tried to look calm, making sure his hair was right. "Excuse me," he said. Burton, without looking up from the note, took one step to his left, away from the technician.

"Good thing the lab has proper ventilation," Gibson said. "Burton, I checked on those two suspects of yours. Neither one of 'em jumps out and screams 'bomber.'"

"I guess that would make your job too easy," Burton said. "What did you find?"

Gibson looked at his notes. "Jack Baker, the former business partner, signed a bad contract with Papa and lost a lot of money. Now he owns Pan's Pizza across town. I asked him about the name, and he said he just wanted something that put him right before Papa's Pizza in the phone book."

"So he has a financial interest in seeing Papa's shut down," Burton said.

"That's correct," Gibson said. "The other guy, Leonard Varney, used to work at Papa's and got caught in some dough-making machine or something. His right hand got pretty messed up and he couldn't work there anymore. He still has all his fingers, but he says the hand isn't nearly as strong as it used to be."

"Sounds like a good reason for revenge," Trellis said.

"You'd have to talk to Radley about that," said Burton. "We need to focus on the *who* and the *how*, not the *why*. This note was written with a manual typewriter; Frank, did you happen to see one when you visited the suspects?"

"Nope," Gibson said.

"We can check the databases to see what kind of make and model was used," Burton said. "When we find the typewriter, we should be able to match it to the letter. Typewriters have a unique fingerprint, with the way they print certain letters a little higher or lower, or maybe a letter has a nick in it that repeats every time it's typed."

"Do you see anything like that in this note?" Trellis asked.

"Well, the first thing that jumps out is that some letters are lighter than others," Burton said, "like the keys weren't pressed as hard. Look here, every time there's an I, L, O, M, P, or N, it's lighter than the other letters."

"What's that tell us?" said Gibson.

"It tells us to arrest Leonard Varney," Burton said. "I think his hands are going to give our case the feet to stand on in court."

How did Burton know?

Burton's File

The lighter letters are a result of the typewriter keys not being pressed hard enough. All of the lighter letters: I, L, O, M, P, and N, are typed using the right hand. Varney injured his right hand in the restaurant accident and did not have the strength to press the keys firmly. Instead of revenge, Varney will be getting jail time.

A Grave Situation

"I don't think there's room for two people in there," Mike Trellis said. He was standing next to the shallow grave in the woods, trying not to let the cold rain get down his collar. Detective Frank Gibson stood next to him in a puffy down parka, the hood hiding his face.

"There already are two people in here," Burton said as he brushed more dirt off the skull. "Besides, if you did some work, you might not be so cold."

"But even if I start removing dirt, the rain just washes it right back in," said Trellis.

"You know what helps?" Gibson said from inside his hood.

"What?" asked Trellis.

"Complaining about it."

"Why don't *you* get in there and start pushing mud around?" Trellis said.

"How long have you had this job?" said Gibson.

"Three years."

Gibson said, "That's why I'm not in the hole: I have seniority. By a few decades. Besides, I see Burton in there with his little shovels and brushes, and it makes me crazy. I'd rather hook the bones to my Chevy and pull them out. Just like a stump."

"Please step away from the hole," Burton said. "Mike,

I'm starting to see some clothing here. Let's get some photos, in case we disturb them later."

"Have any idea who it is?" Gibson said.

"I think I might," Burton said, carefully stepping out of the grave. He looked around to make sure no one was within earshot. Gibson leaned closer, his hood almost touching Burton's face.

"Who?" Gibson whispered.

"Someone with a skeleton," Burton whispered back. Gibson was silent, then said, "I have a hunch that this guy is Donny Chambers. He went missing . . ." Gibson held his notepad in front of his hood, ". . . in 1998. You remember him? He made all that noise about local chemical companies ruining the environment. Then, one day, poof! He's gone."

"I remember," Burton said. "He did those rallies where he had research about the health of people who lived next to the chemical plants. Lots of skin problems, teeth falling out, broken bones all over, bad stuff. Then he talked about how he'd never broken a bone in his life, never been sick. He was right, too; I went through all of his medical records when he went missing."

"Now I'm starting to hope this is him," said Gibson. "It would make him so mad, knowing he was polluting the ground with his own body. What a great joke."

"It could be him," Burton said. "The soil is moist enough to support rapid decomposition, and I can tell by the posterior ramus that it's a male."

"You can tell that by looking at the skeleton's butt?"

Gibson asked, peering into the hole. "But the butt is still buried."

"What?" Burton said. "No. The posterior ramus is the rear part of the jawbone, where it connects with the skull. For females, that part of the bone is straight. For males, it's curved. The one in the grave is curved. What did you say about a butt?"

"Nothing," Gibson said. "How do you know it didn't just break off into a curve?"

Burton got comfortable. "If the break had occurred while the person was alive, there would be a callus at the point of the fracture. A callus is like a scar for your bones; it joins broken pieces together and seals off the edges of a fracture. If the break had occurred at the time of death, it would be rough, maybe even jagged, since the body didn't have time to heal."

Gibson nodded, either because he understood or because he wanted Burton to be quiet. Probably the second one, Burton thought. He pointed at the jawbone, "See how it's nice and smooth? No callus, no fractured edges. This is a male skeleton."

"All right, I got it," said Gibson. "Jeez. Next time remind me to bring a chair."

Burton turned to Trellis, who was standing in the grave to get close-up photos of the skull. "Trade me," he said as he took the camera and handed Mike a small dusting brush.

"Man, you tricked me," Trellis complained, but he got to work removing more soil from the body. "Hey, nice callus on the humerus here," he said, brushing grit away from the whitish line that went all the way around the skeleton's upper arm bone.

Burton leaned in for a closer look. "It's completely healed, so I doubt it has anything to do with the case. Other than to prove that this isn't Donny Chambers."

How did Burton know?

Burton's File

Donnie Chambers's medical records supported his claim that he'd never been sick or broken a bone in his life. The skeleton in the grave had a callus on the humerus, or upper arm bone, the result of the bone healing after a fracture.

A Lie for an Eye

Burton and Mike Trellis walked into the crime lab, Trellis carrying a plastic evidence bag with a human eyeball in it.

"Eye have something for you," he said to Dr. Crown, then spun toward Burton. "Get it? *Eye* have something?"

"I don't see the humor in that," Burton said.

"Good one!" said Trellis, which didn't make Burton happy. If Trellis thought you made a good joke, you were in trouble.

"Is that the mystery eyeball?" Crown asked.

"We found it on the ground next to a burn barrel in Mel Kendall's backyard," Burton said. "Looks like he tried to burn all the evidence of Ray Truman's murder. But we can't prove that yet."

"Guess Kendall doesn't have an eye for detail," Trellis said. He almost couldn't say it, he was laughing so hard.

"Are you sure it belongs to Ray Truman?" Crown asked, ignoring Trellis.

"It matches the color," Burton said, looking at the dark-blue iris. "We can do a DNA comparison to make sure; we got some samples from his wife once he became a missing person. He's been gone for two days now, but who knows how long he's been dead."

"Vitreous humor is fairly resistant to decay," Crown said, referring to the jellylike fluid inside the eyeball. "If he died within the last three or four days, the potassium

119

level in the fluid should give us a good idea of when it happened."

"Do you see the humor in that?" Trellis asked, practically on the floor. "Man, I gotta write these down."

"Please, go do that," Burton said. "Take all day."

"The vitreous humor and the blood are balanced," Crown said, trying to bring some professionalism back into her lab. "So any chemical that is in the blood will also be found in the vitreous humor. But it takes one to two hours for any substance to build up in the vitreous humor after it enters the bloodstream."

"So if I drink a can of soda now," Trellis said, wiping tears from his eyes, "it gets into my blood almost immediately, but my eyeballs won't know I drank it until two hours from now?"

"If you must think of it that way, yes," Crown said. "Of course, it wouldn't be soda once your body breaks it down. It would basically break down to water and fructose, which is very bad for you. We've had this talk about soda before, Michael."

"I know, I know," Trellis said.

"Let me know when you get the test results back," Burton said. "I'm going to see how Detective Gibson is doing with the interview." Burton headed for the door, and Trellis fell in behind him.

"Shouldn't you stay here and help Dr. Crown?" Burton said.

"No," Crown said before the technician could answer.

Burton sighed and continued on, Trellis close behind. Inside the interview room, Mel Kendall had his chair tipped on two legs and he was thumping the back of his head lightly against the wall.

"See? This is what we're doing here," he said. "We're banging our heads against the wall. You arrest me for murder, and you don't even have a dead body. So why are we wasting our time?"

"You want me to show you how to really bang your head against the wall?" Gibson said. "Because what you're doing there, that's nothing."

Burton sat down across from Kendall. "We don't need a dead body to prove murder," he said.

"I beg to differ!" Kendall slammed his chair back onto four legs. "A little something called no *corpus delicti*. No corpse. And without a corpse, there's no murder." He held his hands out to his sides, like there was nothing he could do about how logical he was.

"You've been studying the laws on murder?" Gibson said. "Cramming for Ray Truman's final exam?"

"Nah, I just watch a lot of TV," said Kendall, smiling at the detective.

"Maybe you should have cracked a book," Burton said. "*Corpus delicti* refers to the body of evidence in a case, not the body of the victim."

Kendall stopped smiling.

"So unless Truman is walking around with only one eye," Burton continued, "he's dead. And I have one of the best forensic pathologists in the country examining the other eye right now."

"Look," Kendall said, "the last time I saw Ray was around five o'clock, two days ago. We watched the football game, had some dinner, then he left."

"What'd you have?" Gibson asked. Burton thought the detective's question might have more to do with him being hungry than any police matter.

"I grilled some steaks," said Kendall. "Onions, mushrooms, the works."

"That sounds pretty good," Gibson said, nodding. "Wes, you want some lunch?"

"I think we have time," Burton said and looked at Kendall. "Sit tight; we'll let you know when you should call a lawyer."

During lunch, Burton's cell phone chirped.

"I have Truman's time of death and the possible cause," Dr. Crown said as a greeting.

"Well, hello there, Dr. Crown," said Burton.

"Time of death is at or around 7 P.M. Sunday," she said. "That's yesterday."

"Today is Tuesday, Doc," said Burton. "Sunday was two days ago."

"Fine," she said. Burton could tell that except for the impact it had on the case, she didn't really care what day it was. "I identified traces of a toxin in the vitreous humor I took out of the eyeball. The toxin is from the *Gyromitra* fungus, also called false morel. From the time the poison enters the body, it can be fatal in as little as two hours."

"Thanks, Doc," Burton said. "You just helped me burn Kendall with his own grill."

How did Dr. Crown's findings prove Kendall guilty?

Burton's File

Kendall said he hadn't seen Truman since they ate dinner at 5 P.M. on Sunday, a meal of steak, onions, and mushrooms (fungi) prepared by Kendall. Dr. Crown determined that Truman died around 7 P.M. on Sunday from a fungus toxin that can kill in just two hours. Since the vitreous humor shows traces of what was in the bloodstream two hours earlier, her tests indicate that Truman was poisoned during the 5 o'clock meal.

Behaving in Bad Taste

"I've been assassinated!" Walter Davis said from his bed. Burton and Detective Erin Radley looked at each other.

Radley said, "Mr. Davis, you believe someone tried to kill you? Or have you killed?"

"Precisely!" Davis said. "Someone in the contest wanted me out of the way, and they tried to murder me. But I'm too strong!"

Radley checked her notes. "That would be the 'Annual Jam and Jelly Contest' from yesterday?"

"That's right," Davis said. "I'm the head judge. Obviously, one of the contestants knew I wouldn't pick their jam or jelly, and they decided to kill me for it. Or at least try."

"But you're too strong," said Burton.

"Much too strong," Davis agreed.

"Can you walk us through your day?" Radley said. "It might give us an indication of who to give a closer look."

"Yes," Davis said. "I began my morning with warm water and rice cakes, so as not to spoil my taste buds for the upcoming event. Can you believe Wally actually eats pancakes with syrup on the day of a judging?"

"The nerve," Burton said.

"Indeed," said Davis. "I arrived at the event around 10 o'clock for the judge's parade — my idea — and started tasting the jams around 10:30. I like to taste the jams first, because I find the jellies are better when the sun is warmer."

"Was that all you ate yesterday?" Radley said. "Just the jams and jellies?"

"That's all," said Davis. "I won't even use a cracker or piece of bread to sample them. I get a dollop of the jam or jelly on a plastic plate, and use my finger to taste it."

"Your finger?" Burton said.

"That's right. I find the taste of metal spoons can interfere with the bouquet of flavors the jams and jellies have to offer."

"What about plastic?" Burton said.

"I once cut my tongue on a plastic spoon," Davis said, his gaze drifting away while he remembered the tragic event. His eyes came back to Burton and narrowed. "I will never touch a plastic utensil to my tongue again."

"Okay, take it easy," said Burton. "When did you start to feel the symptoms?"

"Around 11 o'clock last night," Davis said. "I began to experience nausea, cramps, and . . . hmm. What's a nice way to say this?"

"Go ahead," said Radley.

"I had to spend some extra time on the toilet."

"Got it," Burton said. "So the symptoms kicked in about twelve hours after the contest. That could help narrow the list of possible toxins."

"The toilet time was what tipped me off that something

was wrong," Davis said. "I had already used the bathroom during the jam and jelly contest, one of those horrible portable things, and figured I was set for the day."

"Those portable toilets aren't so bad," Burton said, and Radley and Davis both gave him a look. "They even have those hand sanitizer dispensers in there now."

"Goodness, no," Davis said. "That would completely ruin any chance for me to judge the contest. No soaps, no sanitizers."

"So you didn't wash your hands after you used the bathroom?" Radley asked.

"I must not allow any foreign substances to disturb my taste buds," said Davis.

"What about disturbing the people you shake hands with?" Burton said, then turned to Radley. "I'm going to give Dr. Crown a call, to see if she has Davis's test results. If poison is involved, we need to locate the source before anyone else eats it." Burton stepped outside the room and called the crime lab.

Trellis answered, "Mike's Morgue, you kill 'em, we chill 'em."

"Come on, Mike," Burton said. "What if I was the mayor calling?"

"Caller ID, boss," Trellis said.

"Any results on the Davis toxicology?" Burton asked.

"Dr. Crown has ruled out the big players: arsenic, cyanide, mercury, you know. Right now she's testing for several others, but she thinks she's narrowed it down to either botulism or salmonella."

"Food poisoning?" Burton said.

"Makes sense," said Trellis. "You can get botulism from foods that have been improperly heated and canned, and he ate jams and jellies yesterday, right?"

"Yeah," Burton said, "and that's all he ate."

"That probably rules out salmonella then," said Trellis. "You can catch that by eating raw meats or eggs, but it sounds like he didn't have any of that. Dr. Crown said you can also get it by touching a person, animal, or dookie infected with salmonella." Burton heard Dr. Crown say something in the background.

"Sorry," Trellis said. "Not dookie. Feces."

"Thanks for clearing that up," Burton said.

"Here comes Dr. Crown with the results," said Trellis. "And the winner is . . . salmonella! Hey, everybody, how about that?"

"Good job, you guys," Burton said. He hung up and went back into the bedroom. "Get yourself to a doctor and get some antibiotics," he said to Davis. "You have salmonella poisoning."

"I knew it!" Davis said. "When are you going to arrest the villain who tried to murder me?"

"We can arrest him right now if you want," Burton said. "It was you."

How did Davis get salmonella poisoning?

Burton's File

As Trellis said, a person can get salmonella poisoning from coming in contact with an infected person or their feces (also known as dookie or poop). Davis said that he used the portable bathroom at the Annual Jam and Jelly Contest, didn't wash his hands, and continued to use his fingers to sample the jams and jellies. After this case, everything, especially Davis, is going to get a good scrubbing.

Bobbing for Cadavers

The 13-foot boat pulled away from the dock and Mike Trellis immediately looked like he wanted to jump back onto the wooden platform.

"Have you ever tipped this boat over?" he asked the captain, a sheriff named Arnie Johnston.

"Oh, lots of times," Johnston said from his place at the stern, where he held the electric motor on a straight course. A gas motor would pollute the scene with exhaust and oil and could interfere with Ed's nose. He smiled and winked at Burton and Ed. Ed smiled back, her tongue flopping.

"I think I've heard about you," Burton said, sharing the joke. "You're not the same Arnie Johnston who sank the police department's speedboat, are you?"

"That's me," Johnston said. Trellis tried to look back at him from his seat in the middle of the boat, but the two life preservers he wore wouldn't let him turn his head. He started to spin his entire body, but as soon as he lifted his leg the boat tipped in that direction, and he put his leg back down. Forever.

Burton said, "That boat was supposed to be unsinkable."

"I can show you how I did it," said Johnston. "All I had to do was rock the boat one way," he leaned to his left, "then rock it the other way." He went to his right, and the edge of the boat dipped dangerously close to the water.

"Enough!" Trellis squeaked. "Okay, ha-ha, you've had

129

your fun. Now knock it off; Ed's getting scared." Burton looked at Ed, who also had on a life preserver and was having an excellent time watching the minnows zip through the water. "Besides," Trellis said, "we're out here to locate a corpse, not make four new ones."

"You're absolutely right, Mike," Burton said. "We apologize." Burton held his hand up, and Johnston gave him a silent high five.

Johnston said, "So this dog of yours can find Gordon Hill's body under the water?"

"That's right," Burton said, giving Ed a pat. "She can locate the general area that the body is in, then divers go under to retrieve the corpse. It saves a lot of time, and it's a lot safer."

"It's a pretty big lake," Johnston said.

"If he's in here, Ed will find him," Burton said. "Hill's been missing for a week now, and this water is 55 degrees, so his body should be breaking down and giving us plenty of scent to locate."

"What's the water temperature have to do with it?" Johnston asked.

"Warmer water, around 70 degrees, speeds up decomposition and usually makes the body float within a day or so," Burton said. "If the water's cold, say 40 degrees or less, the body could cease all decomposition and stay under water forever, almost perfectly preserved."

"Unless the crabs get to it," Trellis said.

"Good point," Burton said, then turned to Johnston

again. "But even if the aquatic life doesn't get to a body in the water, after a while it can be completely unrecognizable. The face and hands will swell after only two or three days. After three to six months, the fatty tissues in the body turn into a greasy, waxlike substance called adipocere. The fat reacts with the water and basically turns into soap; try identifying a body with soap for a face."

Johnston looked like he wanted to be done learning about bodies in the water, but curiosity got the best of him. He looked at Ed, perched on the bow of the boat with her nose a foot above the water. "So she sticks her nose under the water?" he said. "How does she sniff when she can't breathe?"

"She uses a Scooby tank," Trellis said. He forgot about tipping the boat and tried to turn so he could see everyone crack up. "Get it? Scuba, Scooby?"

"I'm going to push him in," Burton said.

"Quickly," said Johnston. Trellis went back to facing forward, and Burton turned to the sheriff.

"She doesn't have to put her nose under the water," he said. "When a body decomposes under water, it releases oils and other substances that don't break down in water. Instead, they float to the surface and into the air. Ed picks up on that scent and lets me know when we're close."

"I'm surprised we can't smell the body ourselves," Johnston said. "From what you say, it must be pretty ripe."

Burton said, "If the body is floating, we might be able to smell it. But if it's submerged, by the time the odors get to the surface, they're spread out enough that our noses don't detect them. A dog's nose can be a hundred million times more sensitive than ours, so they get all the enjoyment of smelling the corpse."

At first Burton thought Ed was chuffing in agreement, but after the second one he realized that she had located the body. They stopped the boat and radioed the divers, who rode over in another boat and went under.

"Insane," Trellis said, shaking his head as much as he could inside the life preservers.

The divers came back up ten minutes later, pulling a corpse with them. It had a human shape, but other than that didn't really look like a person.

"Advanced adipocere," Burton said as he handed Ed a treat from vest pocket 27 and rubbed menthol balm from vest pocket 29 under his nose. It didn't do much to help the smell.

Johnston looked at the waxy substance covering the body, then looked away. "Man, you were right. That doesn't look a thing like Gordon Hill."

"That's because it isn't," Burton said.

How did Burton know?

Burton's File

The greasy, soaplike substance called adipocere takes at least three months to develop on a submerged corpse. Gordon Hill had only been missing for a week, so the body with advanced adipocere couldn't be him.

Choking on a Lie

"I don't know why I'm still sitting here," Dwayne Vedmore said from the interview room. "I should be in a jail cell."

"You think I'm going to leave you alone once you're in jail?" Detective Frank Gibson said. "Not true. I have a cot in the aisle outside the cells, and sometimes I sleep there so I can bother the inmates all night long."

"It's true," Burton said, sitting across from Vedmore. "His snoring is classified as a form of torture."

"Fine," Vedmore said. "Let's go. I confessed to the murder of Timothy Platt. What more do you need?"

"Proof that you're not a loony," said Gibson.

"Believe it or not, Mr. Vedmore," Burton said, giving Gibson a look, "we get several false confessions for every high-profile case that comes along. And Mr. Platt was a very high-profile man. Whoever murdered him will get plenty of media attention."

"Let's get this straight," Vedmore said. "The cop thinks I'm crazy, and you, whatever you are, you think I'm lying."

"I'm a forensic investigator," Burton said. "And I think you might be both."

Vedmore thought for a moment. "Maybe I am crazy. But if so, I'm a crazy killer, not a crazy liar."

"We should call Radley," Gibson said to Burton. "This fool could take up a whole chapter in her book."

"Can't do it," Vedmore said. "I'm planning to write my

own book on why I killed Platt. They let you have typewriters in prison, right?"

"Yeah," Gibson said. "Right next to your espresso machine and Jacuzzi."

"Maybe we should prove that you killed Pratt before you start decorating your cell," said Burton. He opened the case file and reviewed the facts and photos. Pratt had been killed by strangulation, and several of the photos were close-ups of his neck. A deep, perfectly smooth groove had been left around his throat from the object used to strangle him. "Let's start with how you murdered him."

"I choked him," Vedmore said.

"Can you be more specific?" Burton said, still looking at the file.

"I choked him from behind with a piece of rope."

"That was on all the news channels," Gibson said. "You could have seen it and decided you want some time in the spotlight, so you come down here and confess."

"I have the piece of rope I used," said Vedmore.

Burton looked up. "Where is it?"

"The cop at the front desk took all my stuff," Vedmore said. "It's in a plastic baggie."

"I'll be right back," Burton said, taking the case file with him. As the door closed, he heard Gibson say, "Were you standing behind him like this when you choked him?"

Burton found the desk sergeant, of all places, at his desk. "Do you have Mr. Vedmore's belongings?" The officer flipped through a row of manila pouches and pulled one out.

"Did he do it?" the desk sergeant asked.

"I'm about to find out," Burton said. He opened the pouch and dumped the contents onto the counter. The plastic baggie was there, along with car keys and a wallet, which he moved to the side. The twisted nylon rope inside the baggie was coiled and had a knot at each end to keep the thick strands from unraveling. Burton took the rope and baggie with him for further testing, just to confirm what he already knew, and put the other items back in the pouch.

When Burton entered the interview room, Vedmore smiled.

"Can I go to jail now?" he said.

"Oh, yes," said Burton. "You are certainly under arrest. But for obstruction of justice, not murder. That's what happens when you lie and waste our time."

How did Burton know Vedmore wasn't the killer?

Burton's File

When a killer uses an item to strangle someone, such as a rope, electrical cord, or clothing, they leave a lasting impression — literally. The rope Vedmore claimed he used to strangle Pratt was twisted nylon with thick strands wound around each other.

Whatever Pratt was strangled with, it left a perfectly smooth indentation around his neck; the twisted nylon rope would have left a bumpy groove.

Hit and Run, Right to Jail

"Is this the car from the hit-and-run yesterday?" Burton asked as he entered the crime lab. The car was parked in the garage area, and Mike Trellis was taking close-up photos of the back. Detective Erin Radley watched him.

"We hope so," Radley said. "Ken Hollock, who owns the car, says he didn't hit the guy. But with a hit-and-run, what do you expect?"

"Looks like the car took some serious damage," said Burton, leaning toward the front of the car. "The grille's all smashed in, and the hood has a nice big dent in it. The bumper looks okay, though."

Trellis said, "Well, they're made to hit other bumpers, not people."

"Have you found anything that indicates this is the right car?" Burton asked him.

"Not so far," Trellis said. "But I auto pretty soon. Get it? Auto, ought to? Because this is an automobile." Trellis waited. "Anybody?"

"Start looking for another job," Burton said, then turned to Radley. "How is Jennings doing?"

"He's still in intensive care," Radley said. "It's a real shame. The kid's on a full track scholarship to the University of Omaha, and he comes home for the summer and gets hit from behind by a car while he's walking down the road. The doctor doesn't know if he'll be able to run again."

"I read about him in the paper last year," Burton said. "He set all kinds of state records, right?"

"Just about all of them," said Radley. "He stopped by the high school yesterday, just before he got hit, and gave some pointers to the kids who were doing their off-season workouts there. They all wanted their picture taken with him holding his university jacket in front of him, the great big 'Omaha Huskies' written on the back in all capitals, like it's being shouted."

Burton said, "I already checked the jacket for traces of paint from the car. Nothing. I think the material is too soft to have scraped the paint. Do they have huskies in Omaha?"

"I'll look into it," Radley said. "But first I'd like to find out if Ken Hollock is the one who ran into Jennings."

"Coming right up," Burton said and snapped on a pair of latex gloves. "Mike, did you check the surface of the car for any traces of hair, fabric, skin . . . ?"

"Twice," Trellis said. "The car's been cleaned very well, so I'd be surprised if we find any trace evidence that we can link to Jennings."

"How did Hollock explain the damage to his car?" Burton asked Radley.

"He says he hit a deer," she said. "But it was okay and ran off into the woods, which is possible, I suppose. I asked him where it happened, so you could go out and look for skid marks, deer blood, that kind of thing."

"Thanks, I appreciate that," Burton said. "What did Hollock say?"

Radley said, "He said he couldn't remember where it happened. I guess he runs into deer all the time, and it's hard to keep the details straight. I asked him why he cleaned his car before he reported it to the insurance company, and he said, 'Was that wrong?'"

"Mr. Innocent, huh?" Burton said, crouching in front of the car's grille. "Well, I don't see any fur or blood, so if he did hit a deer, he did a mighty fine job of cleaning."

"I told you," Trellis said.

"You didn't tell me there was an impression in the hood," Burton said, eyeing the dented metal from his crouch.

"What?" Trellis said and bent down next to him.

"See there, in the middle of the dent?" Burton said. "There are shapes imprinted in the metal, very faintly, from the impact of whatever the car hit. It happens sometimes with collisions, where a pattern from the item struck can transfer to the vehicle."

Trellis said, "Oh, yeah. Where I was standing, the light was shining straight down, and you can't see it from there."

"Let's get some other lighting on this, maybe we can make out what the shapes are," said Burton.

"Lighting?" Radley said.

"It's like when you have a pad of paper," said Burton. "If someone writes something and tears the sheet off, you can sort of see what was written by looking at the sheet underneath, because it has an impression. If you shine a light across the page from different angles, the impressions are much more defined. This is the same concept."

Trellis said, "Except this is metal, not paper, and we're looking for the impression of a person. Other than that, it's the same." He turned off the overhead lights and put a flashlight next to the hood of the car so that it went left to right.

"It looks like letters," Radley said.

"A . . . ham . . ." Trellis said, trying to make them out. "I think it says 'A HAM.' Hollock claims he hit a deer, right? Not a pig?"

"No matter what he said, he's lying," Burton said. "He hit Calvin Jennings."

How did Burton know?

Burton's File

Calvin Jennings was wearing his college jacket when he was struck by the car, and the jacket had OMAHA HUSKIES written on the back. When Hollock hit Jennings from behind, a partial backward impression of the letters was put into the car's hood. OMAHA spelled backward is AHAMO.

Hung Out to Lie

It was near dark, and Burton and Mike Trellis left the CSI truck outside the CRIME SCENE tape and walked toward Thomas Sinclair's house. Sinclair had been discovered hanging in the basement around 6 o'clock.

"It's too bad they already put their tape up," Trellis said. "Your CRIME SEEN? tape just adds a little something extra to the scene, you know? Like, 'Hey, somebody died here, but it wasn't you, so tell us what you saw.'"

"That's what I was going for," Burton said. He saw Detective Frank Gibson standing in the doorway waiting for them.

"They did it before I got here," Gibson said.

"Oh, no," said Burton. "What did they do? Don't tell me they cut down the body."

"They cut down the body," Gibson said.

Burton stopped. "Seriously?"

"Seriously."

"Did you fire anyone yet?" Burton asked.

"I was waiting for Trellis to get here," said Gibson. "I figured if anyone should be fired, it's him."

"I just got here," Trellis said.

"Yeah, weird, huh?" said Gibson. He looked at Burton. "The EMTs were first on the scene, and they cut the guy down and tried to revive him. Maybe that's their policy, but I could tell he was gone as soon as I stepped in the room."

"Did they mark the rope before they cut it?" Burton asked as he followed Gibson into the house. "We'll need to know which way he was facing, exactly how far his feet were off the ground. . . . Man, why did they have to cut him down?"

"Maybe they didn't want to leave him hanging," Trellis said. "Wait, that was too easy. How about: Maybe they got tired of him hanging around. Get it? Do you see what I did there?"

Burton said, "I see you just volunteered to be the hanging dummy if we need to re-create this scene." The three of them went through the kitchen and turned left to the basement stairway.

"This is what we know so far," Gibson said, heading down the stairs. "Sinclair had some gambling debt, most likely owed some nasty people a lot of money. His girlfriend talked to him on the phone around 4:30, then came over around 6:00 so they could talk about moving to another state. She finds him hanging in the basement, freaks out, calls 911, and the EMTs arrive within ten minutes."

"Nine minutes and twenty-seven seconds," the lead EMT said from the bottom of the basement stairs. His name tag said ROBERT.

"Thanks, Robert," Gibson said. He pointed toward the body of Thomas Sinclair on the floor. "Maybe you can tell the CSIs why you cut the body down."

Robert looked at Burton and Trellis as he snapped off his latex gloves. "When we arrived on-scene, I asked the girlfriend the last time she spoke with or saw Sinclair. She

141

said about an hour and a half ago, so I made the decision to cut him down and check for vital signs. We got a flatline, no pulse, so we attempted CPR."

"We tried for eight minutes," the other EMT said. Her tag said TRISHA.

"You didn't happen to stop and take detailed photographs and video before you cut him down, did you?" Burton asked. Robert looked at Trisha.

"Um, no," Trisha said.

"Just thought I'd ask," said Burton. "Mike, let's start getting those right now, before we have to move anything."

"I'm on it," Trellis said and got to work with the video camera. Burton surveyed the scene, taking in the remainder of the rope still looped around a beam in the ceiling, the milk crate Sinclair had apparently stood on before hanging himself, and the body.

"Not very pretty, is it?" Robert said.

"Evidence isn't usually pretty," Burton said. "But it is beautiful." Robert looked at Trisha again; she shrugged. When Trellis was done with the camera, Burton knelt next to the body near the head. Sinclair had a deep groove in his throat that went just under his Adam's apple and wrapped straight around to the back of his neck. The edge of the groove was inflamed and red.

"Mike, did you get some close-ups of the neck and throat?"

"Sure did," Trellis said.

"We tried not to move the rope when we took him down," Robert said. "But I think it shifted a little when we were doing CPR."

Burton looked at the rope, which was tied in a classic hangman's noose. The knot lay on the floor near Sinclair's left shoulder. Burton pictured Sinclair hanging with the knot pulling up on his neck, pressing against his left ear, and tilting his head to the right. He nudged the noose aside and saw another groove beneath it; the edges of the dented tissue were pale.

"Detective Gibson," Burton said. "Let's start looking for the people who Sinclair owed money. This case just changed from suicide to murder."

How did Burton know?

Burton's File

When a person is hanged, the noose pulls up and leaves an upside-down V-shaped groove on the throat that points up toward the knot. The deep groove with the red edges went straight around Sinclair's neck, indicating that he was strangled to death, not hanged. The red edges show that he was alive when the choking began, and his blood flowed to the damaged throat tissue.

Sinclair did have a second, V-shaped groove, caused by the noose, but it had pale edges, indicating that he was already dead when he was hanged, so his blood did not respond to the trauma.

Inspect the Insects

Burton and Detective Frank Gibson followed Ed through the thick underbrush, trying to find the body of Michael Curry. Burton moved quietly among the branches and weeds, following the jingle of the bells on Ed's vest. He heard a crash behind him, followed by a string of words that he was glad he couldn't quite make out.

"Frank, can you try not to wreck everything you touch? Until we find the body, we don't know what's important to the crime scene."

Gibson plowed his way through a group of saplings and stopped next to Burton, wiping sweat from his entire head. "I got a better idea," he said. "Let's chop down all these trees, cut all the grass, and turn this place into a golf course. Then we'll be able to spot this Curry guy, no problem."

"That might take a bit too long," Burton said. "And it could damage some of the evidence. *Some* meaning *all*."

"What more evidence do we need?" Gibson said. "We have the guy on videotape robbing a bank, let's see" — he checked his watch; it was 8:10 in the morning — "fourteen hours ago. He gets in a shootout with three officers — some very good friends of mine by the way — and they manage to hit him, but not stop him. He gets to his car and manages to drive all the way out here, then dumps his car and runs into the woods just to make my life miserable."

"How do we know it was Curry robbing the bank?" Burton said. "He was wearing a mask."

"He's a bank robber," Gibson said slowly. "That's what they do. They wear masks and rob banks. It's expected. What they shouldn't do is run into the woods, because what happens is they die from their gunshot wounds in the middle of nowhere, and some crazy hikers find the car and report it to us. Then we have to come out here with your dog and walk a million miles until we find the body."

Burton checked the pedometer that kept track of how far they had walked. "It's 4.3 miles."

"Whatever," Gibson said. "Hey, your dog's back. Maybe it agrees with me."

"Ed is a she," Burton said. "And when she comes back like this, it means she's found the body. Try not to step on it, okay?"

Gibson slapped a mosquito on his neck and looked at the mess in his palm. "I think I just lost a pint of blood." He looked at Burton. "Let's get this over with."

They walked another forty yards before they found the body, Ed leading them right to it. Burton gave her a treat from vest pocket 27 and told her she was very smart and good, and she gave him a look that said, "I know" while she crunched the treat.

"Ugh," Gibson said. "How can anyone eat after looking at that body?"

"She's a professional," Burton said. "She knows her job's done, and it's time to relax. You and I, on the other hand, are just getting started. Which would you like to do, examine the body or take notes?"

Gibson already had his notebook out.

Burton said, "I figured," and checked his watch. "Legal time of death, 8:18 A.M. Estimated time of death?" Burton looked at the body. "It won't do much good to get the body temperature in this heat and environment. We'll say twelve hours ago for now. Dr. Crown might be able to narrow it down for us later."

"That puts his death at around 8 P.M. last night," Gibson said, "two hours after the bank robbery. Sounds about right. Why did you guess twelve?"

"The insect activity," said Burton. "And it's not just a guess, it's an educated guess. When a body dies in the right environment, like this one, it only takes ten minutes for flies to arrive and lay eggs. Those eggs hatch into maggots after twelve hours, and they feed on the soft tissues. I see plenty of maggots. Don't you?"

"Yeah, I see them," Gibson said, not looking at the body.

"After 24 to 36 hours," Burton said, "beetles arrive to feast on the skin. At the 48-hour mark, spiders, mites, and millipedes show up to snack on the bugs that are stuffed from the buffet. It's a very consistent and accurate pattern."

"That's fantastic," Gibson said. He looked like he was regretting the bagel with cream cheese he'd eaten on the way.

Burton started to take photos. "I wonder if the insects can tell things about the body they're eating," he said. "Are they munching along, thinking, 'this guy ate way too much garlic last night'?"

Gibson said, "Right now they're probably thinking you should shut up, and I agree with them."

Burton smiled and continued taking photos. "Uh-oh," he said, and leaned in for a close-up of Curry's face.

"What uh-oh?" said Gibson, but he didn't get any closer to see for himself.

"I just got a great picture of a beetle crawling out of his mouth," Burton said. "It's still here if you want to take a look."

"Are you insane?" Gibson said. "A beetle, great. Why is that uh-oh?"

"Because it means there's a bank robber on the loose. When that bank was robbed yesterday, Michael Curry was already dead."

How did Burton know?

Burton's File

In warm weather, the insects that feed on an outdoor corpse arrive like clockwork. Beetles show up between 24 and 36 hours after death. The bank was robbed 14 hours ago, and the presence of beetles on Michael Curry's body indicates that he had been dead at least 24 hours.

It's Snot What You Know, It's What You Can Prove

"I'd like to help you cops out, but what can I tell you?" Trevor Holloway said from his swiveling executive's chair. "I've been here all day." Burton, Mike Trellis, and Detective Erin Radley stood in front of his desk; Holloway didn't have any other chairs in his office.

"Do you keep your guests standing up to show that you're in charge?" Radley said.

"Hey, I like you," said Holloway, showing teeth that were four shades too white. "You're quick. You like yachts? Let's go out on my yacht tonight."

"I get seasick," Radley said without looking up from her notebook.

"Yeah," Trellis added. "If she sees you in a Speedo, she'll be sick. Get it? *See* sick?"

"Do you work for me?" Holloway asked.

"Um, no," said Trellis.

"Too bad. I'd really like to fire you."

"Mr. Holloway," Burton said, "we have eyewitnesses who say you were at the Sanford Concrete Factory early this morning, planting explosive charges meant to go off tonight."

"So?" Holloway said. "A lot of people know what I look like, and a lot of people don't like me."

"A lot of people are smart," Radley said. Holloway gave her another grin and added a wink.

"Anyway," he said, "my company is in the process of purchasing Sanford Concrete, and they're delaying the sale, being stubborn about some of the equipment. I guess it's been in the family since 1940 or something, and they consider it to be heirlooms. I consider it property, and once I buy the company, it's mine."

Radley said, "Do you need the equipment they want to keep?"

"Of course not," Holloway said. "I'm going to tear the whole place down, build condos. But it's the principle; I'm buying the entire company, not the entire company *except* this thing over in the corner, you get me?"

"Oh, I've got you," Radley said. "Grand sense of self-worth, false charm, manipulative. You're on your way to being classified as a psychopath."

"I've been called worse," Holloway said, dismissing her. He looked at Burton. "Look, I'd never go down to that concrete factory in person. There's all that dust floating around, grit on the floor, people sweating for no good reason." He stood up. "Check this suit out. Peep these shoes. Does it look like I've been creeping around a cement factory?"

"You've had plenty of time to change clothes," Burton said.

"Fair enough, fair enough," said Holloway. "You said you're from the crime lab, right? I watch TV sometimes; it's a 72-inch plasma screen, in case you were wondering. Do you have any forensic proof that puts me there? Any finger-prints, fibers, or — what do they call it — trace evidence?"

"Not so far," Burton said. He tried to remain neutral, relying on facts and data to decide if Holloway was guilty or innocent, but the guy's attitude was getting to him.

"Well, then, I think we're done here," said Holloway.

"How do you know the concrete factory is dusty and gritty?" Radley asked. "You've never been there, right?"

"Sweetheart," Holloway said slowly. "I'm buying the company. I know everything there is to know about it, from the 1982 domestic sales figures to the kind of toilet paper they used yesterday.

"Now if you don't mind, I'm a very busy man," said Holloway. He got up from his chair and walked around the desk, looking at Radley. "If you change your mind about the yacht, don't call, you missed your chance. And you," he slapped Trellis on the shoulder. "Come and work for me so I can fire you." He started to laugh, but it turned into a quick inhalation and ended in a snort. He closed his eyes and stood with his mouth open, completely still.

Trellis looked at him, then at Burton, who shrugged. By the time they realized what was happening, it was too late. Trellis managed to get his notebook binder up to his chin, but Holloway's thundering sneeze still sprayed across his hands and face. Trellis froze, a light mist of spittle dripping down his face.

"No," Trellis whispered.

"Hey, whoo, that was a good one," said Holloway. He watched Burton slip on a pair of latex gloves from vest pocket 5 and gently take the notebook binder away from Trellis. Holloway had covered the back of it in spit and snot from his sneeze. Near the center of the mess was a gray, glistening booger the size of a pencil eraser.

"You can keep that as a souvenir," Holloway said.

"I think I will keep it," Burton said. "But as evidence."

How can Holloway's booger be used prove him guilty or innocent?

Burton's File

The mucous membranes of the nose produce mucus, also known as snot. This slick substance coats the inside of the nose and traps particles of dust, dirt, germs, and other foreign bits that shouldn't make it into the lungs. The mucus and tiny hairs inside the nose surround these particles, and when the mucus dries, a booger is formed.

Holloway claimed he had never been to the Sanford Concrete Factory, but his gray booger suggested he had recently been in an environment with lots of gray dust. The crime lab will analyze the dust in his booger and determine if it matches the dust in the concrete factory.

On the Trail of Truth

Burton and Mike Trellis walked up the forest trail, Burton in front to take care of any spiderwebs that crossed the path. If Trellis caught one across the face, Burton would hear about it all day.

"Hey, Wes," Trellis said. "Want to know what the weather was like on May third, 1962?" He was walking with his head down, looking at his brand-new digital Pocket Weatherperson.

Burton guessed, "Partly sunny with a slight chance of rain."

"Wrong!" said Trellis. "It was 'partly cloudy with possible showers.'"

"What's the difference between partly sunny and partly cloudy?" Burton said.

"One moment," Trellis said, then scrolled through menus and pushed some buttons. He read from the small full-color screen: "'Partly cloudy implies that clouds cover three- to five-tenths of the sky. Partly sunny indicates that five- to seven-tenths of the sky is covered with clouds.'"

"Branch," Burton said and ducked under the maple limb that stretched over the path at shoulder height.

"Clouds don't have anything to do with branches," Trellis said, still looking at the Pocket Weatherperson. The maple caught him just under the chin. "Gork!"

Burton tried not to laugh but lost the battle. "Maybe you

should put that away and look around," he said. "We spend so much time in the lab and inside warehouses and basements, it's nice to get out here and enjoy nature."

Trellis frowned. "We're out here trying to determine whether or not Eugene 'Crazy Gene' Edwards killed his psychiatrist yesterday afternoon."

"Even so," Burton said. "Hey, look, a finch." They walked farther up the trail, and eventually came to a mid-sized clearing with a large rock beneath a pine tree.

"This is it," Burton said and checked his notebook to make sure he had the details. "Edwards says he was hiking around here all day yesterday, and sat on this rock when it started to rain. When the rain lightened up, he continued up the trail."

"Let's see here," said Trellis. He poked at the buttons and screen for about a minute until he got what he was looking for. "Yesterday the rain started at 1:07 P.M., was a heavy downpour until 2:34, then softened to a light patter until 3:18. Since then, we've had sunny skies with zero precipitation."

"It really tells you all that?" Burton said, leaning over for a look.

"Yes, it does," said Trellis, giving him a flat look. "And it would have told me about that maple branch, too, because it's my friend."

"Hmm," Burton said and went back to his notes. "Dr. Crown put the psychiatrist's time of death at 3:00 P.M. So if Edwards is telling the truth about his hike, he can't be the killer."

"Do you think he got the nickname Crazy Gene before he went to the psychiatrist or after?" Trellis asked.

"That's a question for Radley," Burton said. "But, if I remember correctly, you didn't get the nickname Stinky Mike until after the incident with the overalls."

"I couldn't get the zipper to work!" Trellis said.

"And I told you not to have burritos for lunch," said Burton. "Now put that gadget away and let's start looking for evidence. Remember, Edwards said that he never hikes on trails, so be careful when you're looking."

They set up a search grid and started looking for any indication that Edwards had been at the site. Through thick underbrush and thorns, they looked for the smallest trace.

"Why can't he just stick to the trails?" Trellis complained, picking a thorn out of his hand.

"He may have done us a favor by staying away," said Burton. "On the trail, we have to sort through the tracks, fibers, and traces from all the other hikers. If we find something out here, we can be pretty sure it was him."

Trellis said, "If I see a bear track, I'm gone."

"I'll do my best to find one," Burton said, as he went back to looking for evidence. He thought Trellis might come back with something he considered witty, but instead the technician said:

"Bootprint."

Burton worked his way over to the small clearing and knelt next to the partial bootprint in the dark earth. There were no branches directly above him, and the sun came down to provide plenty of light. He looked closely; the soil around the print was indented from yesterday's heavy rain, and the print from the boot's tread had a few spots where water had hit it and dried.

"Does it match?" Burton said.

Trellis pulled an actual-size photo of Edwards's boot print out of his satchel and compared it to the print in the dirt. "It matches," he said. "But all that means is that Edwards was out here at some time. Who knows when?"

"Mother Nature does," Burton said. "And she says Edwards didn't kill the psychiatrist."

What proves that Edwards is innocent?

Burton's File

The Pocket Weatherperson stated that the rain came in "a heavy downpour until 2:34, then softened to a light patter until 3:18." The soil around the bootprint showed the effects of the heavy rain, but the soil under the print had only a few drops of water. This means that the print was made when it was only raining lightly, between 2:34 and 3:18.

If it was made before 2:34, during the downpour, the track would show more effects from the heavy rain. If Edwards had walked there after 3:18, when the rain was done, the track would have no drops within its treads. The psychiatrist was murdered at 3:00, while Edwards was hiking peacefully through the woods.

Privy to the Proof

Bug was waiting for them outside the apartment complex, sitting on the back bumper of his Sensitive Cleaners van. Burton and Mike Trellis parked the CSI truck but didn't get out right away.

"What's he eating?" Trellis asked, watching Bug smile at them through the windshield, his mouth full of food.

"I think it's some kind of pastry," said Burton. "I'm not sure."

"You don't think he found that at the crime scene, do you?" Trellis asked.

Burton said, "If he did, we're going to have a hard time getting it back. Look how happy he is." They got out of the truck and walked over to Bug, who stood up and extended the hand that wasn't holding the mystery food.

"Burtons, Mikes, is good you are here," Bug said with a stuffed cheek. They shook hands while he swallowed. "Mmm. This is tasty. Would you like some?" He held the lumpy item in front of them.

"Wes would," said Trellis. Bug smiled and offered the thing to Burton, who smiled back and took a bite.

"Oh, man," he said. "You're right, Bug, that is mighty tasty. Mike, you have to try this."

"Really?" Trellis said. He held the possible sandwich to his nose and gave it a sniff. "Smells like feet."

"Trust me," Burton said. Trellis paused for a moment,

squinting at Burton, then chomped down. He chewed twice, then handed the suspicious food back to Bug and let the bite fall out of his mouth onto the ground.

"Flah! That's the worst thing I've ever tasted!"

"I know," Burton said, laughing. "Isn't it horrible?"

"What are you talking about?" Bug said, looking sadly at the wasted bite on the ground. "This is my own recipe for energy bar. It has onion, egg, maple syrup, garlic, bologna, and one half banana."

"It gave me just enough energy to run to the toilet," Trellis said.

Bug snapped his fingers. "Toilet is why I called you here," he said. "I am cleaning apartments of droppings from vermin, and I find speck of blood behind toilet. So I spray with the luminol, like you show me, Burtons."

"I didn't show you that so you could do it yourself," said Burton.

Bug waved him off. "I just spray a little, to see if I need to charge for blood cleanup, too. But after I spray, the blood is everywhere. Someone tried to clean it up, but did poor job, very unprofessional. Then I call you."

"Let's go take a look," Burton said. The apartment was on the ground floor, and the manager was waiting for them at the door, along with a uniformed police officer who'd arrived before the CSI team.

The nervous manager introduced herself as Tina Blain. "This apartment has been empty for a few months," she said, her hands grabbing at each other. "I've been using it as a model to show possible tenants. You know, so they can see how it looks without someone else's furniture and mess. Do you really think somebody was killed in there?"

"It could be they just had a nosebleed," Burton said, trying to calm her down.

"Oh, no," said Bug. "Is much too much blood for that."

Burton gave him a look, then said, "Miss Blain, we don't even know if the blood is human yet." She relaxed a bit, then looked at Bug, who was nodding that he was certain it was human. Burton saw it, too. "Get inside," he said. "And don't spray any more luminol."

When Trellis and Bug were inside the apartment, Burton said, "Sorry about that, Miss Blain. You mentioned that the apartment has been empty for several months. Has anyone else had access to it besides you?"

"Well," she said, "sometimes I leave the door unlocked during the day. I might have a dozen or so possible tenants take a look at it, and it saves the trouble of remembering my keys."

"Could someone sneak inside without you knowing?" Burton asked. "Maybe spend a few hours in there?"

"I suppose," Blain said. "But when someone moves out, we shut off the water to the apartment. Too many evicted tenants who like to leave the water running, you know?" Burton nodded. "So I guess someone could stay in there for a couple hours without me knowing about it, but they wouldn't have any running water. Does that help?" she asked.

"Everything helps," Burton said, "except the stuff that doesn't." He entered the apartment and found Bug and

Trellis outside the bathroom. Trellis had the lights off and was shining an ultraviolet light onto the tiled walls and floor.

"It looks like two people had a blood fight in here," Trellis said, "and both of them lost." The bathroom was spattered with glowing streaks and puddles of blood trace.

"This is going to cost extra," said Bug.

Burton surveyed the room. "I thought you said you only sprayed a little luminol," he said.

"I have five-gallon bucket," Bug said. "After this, only a little is gone."

Burton shook his head. "Mike, we need photos and video of everything. Get some swabs of the blood for testing, and make sure you get samples from several spots so we can determine if this is more than one person's blood. I'll be right back."

"If this all came from one person," said Trellis, "they're either dead or robbing a blood bank."

Bug grabbed the technician's shoulder. "Blood bank! Bah-ha-ha!" Trellis smiled for a moment, but that disappeared when Bug slammed him into the wall during his laughing fit. Burton walked back in as the laughter was ending, then waited, ready to take notes while Trellis recorded the scene. When that was done, he took a pipe wrench from the back pocket of his pants.

"Is that why you had to leave?" Trellis asked. "To get the wrench? I can't believe you don't have one in that vest of yours."

"I do," Burton said, "but it isn't big enough." He

squatted next to the sink and loosened the nuts on the "P" trap, the curved pipe just below the drain that keeps items that fall into the sink from washing away. "I've found things in 'P' traps that would make you brush your teeth outside," Burton said as he removed the pipe. "Eyeballs, fingers, portions of a small intestine . . ."

"I once found a human foot," Bug said. Burton and Trellis both looked at him. Bug shrugged. "It was a big sink."

Burton took his own bottle of luminol out of vest pocket 23 and misted the inside of the "P" trap pipe. Trellis handed him the UV light, and the inside of the pipe fluoresced.

"What are you looking for?" said Trellis. "Some new earrings?"

"No," Burton said. "As of right now, I'm looking for the last tenants in this apartment. They have some explaining to do."

How did Burton know it was the tenants who tried to clean up the blood?

Burton's File

Tina Blain, the apartment manager, said that when a tenant moves out they shut off the water. When the inside of the "P" trap pipe fluoresced, that meant blood had been washed down the drain. Whoever tried to clean up the mess had access to running water.

Scarred of the Evidence

"I want my lawyer," Mitch Blackburn said. Detective Erin Radley, who sat across from him in the interview room, sat back.

"Why do you think you need a lawyer?" she said.

"Because I know you have Burton working on this case," Blackburn said, "and he's tricky. I didn't steal that armored car, but he'll make it look like I did."

"CSI Burton finds the truth," Radley said. "If you didn't steal the armored car, that's what he'll prove."

"Yeah, right," Blackburn said.

Radley said, "You're just mad because he found the evidence that convicted you last time. How long were you in prison?"

"Two years," said Blackburn.

"All because of a little piece of fabric you tracked in with your shoe," Radley said. "Did you enjoy your stay at the correctional facility?"

Blackburn held up his hands to show the scars that laced across his palms and fingers. White lines crisscrossed each fingertip. "It was a blast," he said. "Some maniac thought I wanted to steal his toilet, so he tried to turn me into smaller pieces of myself." He looked at his hands. "I couldn't pick anything up for weeks. You know how hard it is to brush your teeth with sliced-up fingers?"

"No," Radley said. "So you've been out of prison for six months now. Why did you go back to armed robbery?"

"Now you're the tricky one," Blackburn said. "I told you, I didn't rob the armored car."

"Mmm-hmm," Radley said. "You know, scars are interesting. Some cultures think they're ugly and ought to be covered or repaired, and some think they're symbols of bravery and should be displayed with pride."

"Yeah?" Blackburn said, rubbing his thumbs over the thin white scars on the tips of his fingers. "I'd be the bravest guy in town."

"I'm thinking about putting a section about it in my book," said Radley. "It would focus on the psychology of scars. One theory states that scars are our body's way of telling us we screwed up, and shouldn't do that again."

Blackburn frowned.

"Say a lion is chewing on a bone," Radley said. "You try to take it away, and the lion bites your hand. Every time you see those scars, you're going to think, 'Let the lion have the bone.' It's a constant lesson on how not to get bit again."

"But I didn't get bit by a lion," Blackburn said. "I got cut by a guy protecting his toilet. Which I didn't even want."

"Did you want the money in the armored car?" Radley said.

Blackburn paused. "Nice try," he said. There was a knock on the door and Burton stuck his head in.

"Hello, Erin," he said. "Hi, Mitch. Nice to see you."

"Beat it," Blackburn said, still looking at his scars.

Burton leaned in for a closer look, his eyebrows raised. "Erin, can I see you in the hall?" Radley stepped out and closed the door. "It looks like we found a single fingerprint on the rearview mirror of the armored car. Mike is taking photos right now, then I'll lift the print and check it against Blackburn's. Shouldn't take too long."

"Sounds good," Radley said. "We're having an interesting discussion about scars. What's your opinion about them?"

"Well, when the skin is damaged," Burton said, "scab formation starts almost immediately. Cells begin to regenerate after about thirty-six hours, and if the wound is deep enough, the —"

"Never mind," Radley said as she went back into the interview room. Burton shrugged and headed back to the crime lab, where Trellis was finishing with the photos.

"Ready for liftoff," Trellis said. "Get it? Because you're going to lift the print off the mirror."

"Go take some pictures of the bottom of a lake," Burton said, pulling on a pair of latex gloves. He eased into the driver's seat of the armored car and took his lifting tapes out of vest pocket 7, a small flashlight from 8, fingerprint brushes from 16, and a container of silver latent print powder from 22.

He pointed the flashlight at the rearview mirror from different angles until the beam caught the ridges of the fingerprint. He made a mental note of where it was, then picked up the fingerprint brush and twirled it between his palms to fluff out the bristles.

Trellis watched him dip the tip of the brush into the print powder, then gently dust it over the print on the mirror in the direction of the print, going from the bottom up. Burton looked at it closely, then lightly blew on it to remove any extra powder. He placed the left edge of the lifting tape against the mirror and rolled it onto the print, putting the dark loops and whorls in the exact center of the tape.

"Nice placement," Trellis said.

"I've been doing it a while," said Burton. He pressed the tape down to make sure it picked up every detail, then lifted the tape in one smooth motion. Any hesitation in the lift would leave lines in the print and ruin the evidence.

Trellis gave him a white lift card that he'd already labeled with the date, time, and location of the print. Burton pressed the tape onto the card, reviewed the notes, and initialed it. He handed it to Trellis, who admired the flawless swirls and arches of the print.

"This one's a keeper," he said. "Let's run it through the system and see who pops up."

"I can tell you who it won't be," said Burton. "Mitch Blackburn."

How did Burton know?

Burton's File

The print lifted from the armored car's mirror was flawless; Blackburn had scars across each of his fingertips, and any fingerprint he left would have had lines, creases, and other signs of the damaged fingertips.

164

Shooting for the Truth

"I thought I was done with all of this," Dustin Ray said, sitting in the interview room. He looked from Burton to Detective Frank Gibson. "I mean, the shooting was ruled as justified, right?"

"That's right," Gibson said. "You're not here to talk about the burglar you shot and killed last month. But if you want to tell the story, I'll listen. I especially like the ending."

Ray looked at Burton. "Is he serious?"

"Almost never," Burton said. "Mr. Ray, what can tell us about the gun you used to shoot the burglar?"

"My gun?" Ray said. "It's a .32 caliber Smith and Wesson. You ought to know, you guys haven't given it back yet." Gibson paced behind his chair. Ray kept looking back, first over his left shoulder, then his right.

"That's why you're here," Burton said. "We ran ballistics tests on the gun, standard procedure in any shooting, and —"

"What's a ballistics test?" Ray said.

"Well," said Burton, "we had to make sure that the bullet in the dead burglar actually came from your gun, so we fired some test rounds and compared them to the slug we extracted from his body."

"Compared what?" Ray said. "Like, the manufacturer? Because I buy bullets from lots of places."

"Like to shoot, don't you?" Gibson said without breaking stride.

"Yeah, target practice," said Ray, and Gibson barked a laugh.

"To answer your question," Burton said, "when a bullet is fired and passes through a gun, the gun leaves marks on the bullet. Those marks will be the same for every bullet fired from that gun. The marks on the test slugs matched the one from the burglar, so we were able to determine that he was shot with your gun."

"I know," Ray said. "I was the one who shot him."

"And who else have you shot?" Gibson said.

"What?" Ray said, trying to find the detective behind him.

"Mr. Ray," said Burton. "We also submitted the test bullets to the FBI's General Rifling Characteristics File, and they came back with a match."

"What does that mean?" Ray said.

"It means you shot at least four other people, buddy," Gibson said, leaning over his shoulder.

"You're crazy!" Ray said.

"Maybe," said Gibson. "In fact, most likely, but that doesn't change the fact that you're a killer."

Ray looked at Burton, his eyes huge. "What's he talking about?"

"The FBI database matched the bullets we fired from your gun with slugs taken from four other fatal shootings," Burton said. "Records show the gun has been registered to you for the past ten years, is that right?"

"Yeah," Ray said, looking like he might be sick.

"The shootings all took place five years ago," said Burton. "Was the gun in your possession at that time?"

"I guess, but this isn't right," Ray said. "I never shot anybody before that burglar. Just the paper targets down at Big Dan's Gun Shop and Shooting Range."

"Yeah, practicing for hunting the big game, right?" Gibson said.

"No!" Ray said. "I just shoot because it's fun, not for competition or anything. You can ask Big Dan; he sees me there all the time. He sold me the gun and even fixed it when the barrel cracked last year."

"How did he fix it?" Burton asked.

"Put a new one on, I guess," Ray said.

"We're very sorry for this inconvenience, Mr. Ray," Burton said. "You can go, but I'm afraid you're going to have to find a new place to shoot, because Big Dan is going to jail."

How did Burton know?

Burton's File

When a bullet is fired, the only portion of the gun that it comes in contact with is the inside of the barrel. The barrel has grooves in it to make the bullet spin, and these grooves create unique marks.

Even though Dustin Ray owned the gun for the past ten years, Big Dan replaced the barrel last year. The gunshop owner took the barrel off the gun used in those four shootings and put it on Dustin Ray's pistol.

The Angle of Guilt

"Dude, somebody, like, shot at me," Russell Smith said inside his dirty ground-floor apartment. He brushed the long hair out of his eyes to get a better look at Burton, Mike Trellis, and Detective Frank Gibson. He gave it a few seconds, then let the hair fall back.

"Like, really?" said Gibson. "Did they, like, shoot at you, or did they just plain shoot at you?"

"Yeah," Smith said.

"I'm starting to see why," said Gibson.

Smith said, "I was jamming out on my guitar, really rocking it, and when I was done, I look over and there's this hole going through my refrigerator."

Burton walked over to the appliance and looked at it. The bullet had gone into the left side, through the food area, and exited the right side. "Mike, let's get some pictures of this."

"Did the bullet hit anything good in there?" Trellis asked with the camera pressed against his eye.

"My gallon of milk, man," said Smith.

"Maybe the milk had gone bad," said Trellis. "Get it?"

Smith looked at him for ten seconds. "Hey, man, that's a good title for my song!" He picked up his electric guitar and made some noise with it, then started singing. "Oh, the milk's gone bad! The butter, she's not glad! The cookies know that they're had! The —"

"Enough!" Gibson shouted and pulled the plug out of the guitar.

Burton waited until the last chord faded. "Did the person only fire once?"

"I guess," said Smith, catching his breath. "Like I said, man, I was jamming. I didn't hear a thing."

"Is there anybody, besides me," said Gibson, taking out his notebook, "who would want to shoot you?"

"The dudes in the building across the street are always hollering at me," Smith said. "Telling me to knock off the racket, throw my guitar away."

"Well," Burton said, "the bullet holes do indicate the shot came in through the window that faces the apartment building across the street." He traced a path with his finger from the window to the refrigerator, through one side and out the other. "We could check the guys across the street for gunshot residue."

"If they didn't wash it off already," said Gibson. He looked at Smith. "What time did this happen?"

Smith looked at his wrist, which did not have a watch on it. "About three, I guess."

"Three in the afternoon?" Gibson said. Smith nodded. "It's only 1:30 right now. Did you see into the future?"

Smith shook his head. "Three o'clock yesterday, man," he said.

Gibson paused. "Somebody shot at you yesterday, and you didn't report it until today?"

"Man, I was *jamming*!" Smith said. Gibson threw his notebook into the garbage.

Burton said, "That doesn't give us much hope for finding gunshot residue. Mike, if you have all the photos, let's check the angle of the bullet's path."

They inserted a rod into the entrance hole on the left side of the refrigerator, ran it through the inside, and pushed it out the exit hole on the right. Burton took a tape measure from vest pocket 13 and checked the height of the entrance hole.

"It's 36 inches," he said, and Trellis recorded it. Burton walked around to the exit hole and checked the height. "And this is 24 inches."

"Those two guys who don't like you," Gibson said to Smith, "which apartments do they live in?"

"Um," Smith said. "I think one dude lives on the ground floor, like me, and the other dude lives on the second floor. It's funny when they're both yelling at the same time, man. It's, like, the beginning of *The Brady Bunch*, everybody all stacked on top of each other, looking around."

"I'll be sure to put that in the report," said Gibson.

"When you're done with that," said Burton, "let's go question the guy on the second floor."

Why did Burton suspect the man on the second floor?

Burton's File

The bullet's entrance hole was 36 inches high, and the exit hole was 24 inches high. That puts the bullet on a downward angle, indicating that it was fired from a spot higher than the refrigerator.

If the suspect who lived on the ground floor had fired the bullet, it would have entered and exited the refrigerator at a flat angle, since he would be shooting straight across.

The Bloom of Doom

Burton and Detective Erin Radley were at the Schumann house to collect samples from the bedroom where Larry Schumann had died.

"You have your work cut out for you," Radley said.

"Tell me about it," said Burton. "I see vomit, diarrhea, more vomit, and I think that might be drool over there in the corner."

"Human?" Radley asked.

"We'll test everything to make sure," said Burton, "but I don't know any animals who would hang out in the room while all this was going on. Broken lamps, tables turned over . . ."

Radley said, "You think there was a struggle?"

"Maybe," said Burton, "but it was Larry struggling with himself. It looks to me like he had some kind of seizure and tore the place up while he churned out various fluids."

"Pleasant," Radley said. "His wife said he didn't have any health problems, and I checked his medical records. Nothing that would cause a seizure."

"Mike and Dr. Crown are performing the autopsy right now," said Burton. "Maybe they'll find something, some kind of toxin, and we can locate the source here."

"Toxin?" Radley said. "You suspect Larry was poisoned?"

"I suspect everything and everyone right now," Burton said.

"Until we find some evidence, I have no opinion." He stooped down and collected a sample of vomit from the floor, then scraped it into an evidence bottle from vest pocket 10.

"I'll go talk to Mrs. Schumann some more," said Radley. "I think she's out in the yard. Unless you need some help?"

"Actually, if you could —" Burton turned to her with a bottle and a swab, but she was already gone. "I can't believe I'm saying this," he mumbled to himself, "but I wish Mike was here."

Burton's cell phone chirped and he took it out of vest pocket 18. "Burton," he said.

"Wes, this is Mike."

"Hey, Mike, I was just thinking about you."

"I didn't do it," Trellis said.

"Of course you did," said Burton. "Have you and Dr. Crown found anything yet?"

"We think so," said Trellis. "Schumman had toxins in his system. It looks like he was poisoned by eating part of an azalea plant. I can put Dr. Crown on the line, and she can explain how it modifies the sodium channels of the cell membranes."

"Don't do that," Burton said. "I only have two hours of battery time left on my phone. So Schumann had parts of an azalea plant in his stomach?"

"That's where it gets tricky," Trellis said. "All we could

174

find in the digestive tract is some coffee and what seems to be some kind of honey cake."

"What if he just ate one leaf by mistake?" Burton asked. "Would that be enough to kill him?"

"It's possible," said Trellis. "You see, Wes, when the body ingests . . . oh, here comes Dr. Crown. She knows I have no idea what I'm talking about."

"CSI Burton?" Dr. Crown said through the phone.

Burton said, "Yes, Dr. Crown," trying to sound formal.

"The entire plant is toxic," she said, "so it wouldn't matter what part Larry Schumann ate. It could have been the blossom, the stem, the leaf. Even if he made tea out of the leaves, he'd still get the poison. Any substance made from the plant will contain the toxin."

"Got it. Thanks, Dr. Crown," Burton said. "Can you put Mike back on for a second?" He heard the phone shift around.

"Yes?" Trellis said.

"I just wanted you to know that while you're there in the air-conditioned lab, poking at a nice clean dead guy, I'm standing in a lake of vomit and diarrhea."

"Ah," Trellis said. "A room with a spew? Get it? Instead of a room with a view? Hello?"

Burton hung up and walked outside. Radley was standing with Mrs. Schumann, who was wiping tears away.

"At least he had his favorite dessert the night before he died," Mrs. Schumann was saying to Radley. "He always loved my homemade cakes. Honey cake especially, because

I use honey from Larry's beehive out back." She looked off, remembering something, and the tears came again.

"Mrs. Schumann," Burton said, trying to speak softly, "do you have any azalea plants on your property?"

"Yes, over in the garden," she said, a puzzled look on her face. Radley seemed just as confused. "Why do you ask?"

"I just want to check something," Burton said. "Can we take a look at them?" He and Radley followed her into the garden, where she pointed to a large evergreen shrub with purplish flowers.

"There's the azalea," Mrs. Schumann said. Burton walked closer, looking for any cut branches or missing leaves that might explain the toxins in Larry's body. A bee buzzed next to his left ear and he leaned away from it as another one swooped in from the right and landed on his vest.

"Oh, don't worry about them," Mrs. Schumann said. "Larry's bees are harmless. But, my goodness, they love that bush. I would, too, if I were a bee; look at all the pretty flowers."

Burton looked at the blossoms on the shrub, and saw that dozens of bees were busy collecting nectar. "Well, for being harmless and pretty," he said, "they managed to team up and commit a murder."

How did Larry Schumann die?

Burton's File

Dr. Crown said that any substance made from the azalea plant would contain the poison. Larry's honeybees made honey using nectar collected from the azalea, and Mrs. Schumann used that honey to make the honey cake. Mrs. Schumann didn't know that she poisoned her husband with his favorite dessert.

The Foul Home Run

Burton and Ed the border collie got to the high school baseball field just as the second inning started. He found Mike Trellis standing next to the bleachers along the first baseline.

"Did I miss it?" Burton said.

"No," said Trellis. "Aaron got a double his first time up, and he's on deck right now for his second at-bat." Aaron was Trellis's cousin, who needed one more home run to break the school record.

Burton looked around. "Pretty good crowd. And a nice day for baseball."

"Yeah, maybe a little too hot," Trellis said and wiped his brow. "It has to be close to 90 degrees. But look at Aaron, not even sweating."

"Cool kid," Burton said, and opened the thermos of water he had under his arm. It had a rack on the side for plastic cups, and he pulled out two. "You want some water, Ed?" he asked, and she showed him her pink tongue. "I guess that means yes."

"I'll take some too," Trellis said, then yelled, "Come on, Aaron! Smack it outta here!"

"He's not even up yet," said Burton.

Trellis said, "I know. But when he is, everyone will be yelling it. I wanted to be sure I'm heard."

"Hmm," Burton said. Trellis took a sip of his water and

looked for a place to put the cup. He looked at the head of a short man standing next to him.

"Don't do it," Burton said.

"He's wearing a hat," Trellis said. "I could put my cup on top of his head and he'd never know."

"Just set it on the ground," Burton said.

Trellis did, putting it a few inches away from Ed's cup, which was still about half full. The home crowd was yelling for the batter, Lyle, to get a hit.

"Come on, Lyle!" Trellis said. "Get it in play now, Lyle!" He looked at Burton.

Lyle hit a pop fly to shallow left field and trotted back to the dugout. "Hey, Aaron's up," Trellis said. "I think I'm more nervous than he is." He bent down to get his water and saw the two cups next to each other. "Aw, man. I forgot which one is mine."

"Does it matter?" Burton said.

"Well," Trellis looked at Ed, who looked back and waited for his answer.

"Her mouth is cleaner than yours," Burton said.

"Yeah, but," Trellis said, then whispered, "what if she ate something disgusting recently?"

"She didn't."

Trellis looked at the cups, then Ed, then Burton. Then the cups again.

"Fine," Burton said. He pulled his handheld ultraviolet light out of vest pocket 25. He swept it over the two cups, and the one on the left had several splotches that glowed under the purplish light. "There you go. There's saliva all over the one on the left, so unless you slobber more than Ed, yours is the cup on the right."

"Thanks," Trellis said and picked up his water. "No offense, Ed."

Burton said, "Notice she wouldn't drink out of your cup, either."

The crowd cheered while Aaron walked up to the plate, everyone yelling encouragement and getting anxious to see if this would be the at-bat to break the record. It got quiet as Aaron dug in at the plate, got his feet right, and took a few practice swings.

The pitcher pulled his cap down and stared at the catcher, nodded once and licked his fingers. He had the ball in his glove and worked on it, getting his grip just right, then went into his windup and threw the first pitch.

"Ball!" the umpire yelled. The crowd clapped, but it wasn't what they wanted. The pitcher got the ball back and went through the same routine, nodding at the catcher, licking his fingers, and gripping the ball. He took a deep breath, wound up, and threw.

"Ball two!"

"Pitcher's not giving him anything to hit," Trellis said.

"Can you blame him?" said Burton. "He's here to win the game, not serve up the record-breaking pitch."

"Still," Trellis said. "I wish he'd just put something over the plate and get it over with. Can't he see how nervous I am?"

"You're right," Burton said. "How can he be so selfish?"

The pitcher was into his routine again, licking his fingers and working the ball. He picked up his leg, drew back, and hurled a fastball right down the middle. The crack of the bat rolled over the crowd as they jumped to their feet, and the ball sailed out, out, out into the tall grass beyond the center-field fence.

"Yes!" Trellis yelled. Aaron jogged around the bases, getting high fives from the base coaches, and met his entire team at the plate. They pounded him on the back and helmet, jumping up and down while he grinned and touched home.

Trellis said, "Oh, I feel so much better now."

"That was a bomb," Burton said, looking out at the weeds where a crowd of people was looking for the record-setting ball. "Hey, Ed, wanna go find a ball?" Ed's tail swished back and forth, and she headed toward the tall grass with Burton and Trellis. By the time they arrived, there were close to twenty people looking for the baseball.

"Ed, where's the ball?" Burton said, and she took off, rustling through the dry weeds.

"Does that work with car keys?" Trellis asked.

"I wish," Burton said.

"I found it!" a man yelled, and stood up with the ball raised above his head. The other people in the field either cheered or groaned and started back toward the bleachers.

"Good job, man," Trellis said. "That baby's going to look great in the trophy case."

"Trophy case?" the man said. "Naw, I'm gonna keep this ball."

"Keep it?" Trellis said. "What for? You didn't hit it."

"But it's a record breaker," the man said. "I might even sell it online. Somebody's gotta be willing to pay for it, right?"

"No, no," said Trellis. "My cousin hit that ball. If anyone should keep it, it's him."

"What's he willing to pay?" the man said. "Bidding starts at fifty bucks."

"Fifty bucks!" Trellis said. "Are you insane?"

"Hold on," Burton said, seeing that Trellis was about to blow a gasket. "We don't even know if this is the right ball."

"Of course it is," the man said. "Do I hear fifty-five?"

Trellis gritted his teeth and growled.

"Mike," Burton said, "can you go find Ed? I think she went that way. I'll stay here and check out this ball." Trellis turned away and thrashed through the weeds, muttering about how someone should buy some manners online.

"Okay, he's gone," the man said. "I'll sell it to you for forty, but don't tell anyone."

"Let me see the ball," Burton said.

"Let me see the money."

Burton sighed. "Can you at least hold it out and spin it for me? I want to check something."

The man eyed him for a moment. "I guess," he said. "But don't try anything funny."

"Oh, this is already funny enough." Burton reached into pocket 25 again and brought out the UV light.

"What's that?" the man said.

182

"It's a death ray," said Burton.

"Nuh-uh."

Burton swept the light around the baseball, making sure he checked the entire surface. The ball didn't have any spots that illuminated under the UV. He clicked the light off.

"Forty bucks," the man said. "What do you say?"

"I say you found the wrong ball."

How did Burton know?

Burton's File

Saliva, like the drool on Ed's water cup, will glow under ultraviolet light. The ball found in the field did not have any glowing spots, but the home run ball would; before every pitch, the pitcher licked his fingers and gripped the ball, putting traces of his saliva on the ball.

The Haunted House's Gory Details

"Thirty minutes waiting in line," Detective Frank Gibson said. "This had better be good." It was the night before Halloween, and the whole crew was at the Realm of Terror Haunted House. Burton had planned the trip to help the team blow off some steam.

"The advertisement claimed it's the scariest haunted house in the state," Burton said. "But the ads for all the other haunted houses claimed the same thing, so who knows?" He looked at Trellis. "Have you heard anything about this one, Mike?"

Trellis had his eyes closed and was taking deep breaths. Burton put his hand on the technician's shoulder. "Mike?"

"Geeya!" Trellis screamed. "What are you trying to do, kill me?" He pointed at the poster next to the ticket counter. "I'm about to walk into a 'horrifying realm of terror!' I need some time to collect myself!"

Burton looked at Dr. Crown, who was peering closely at a mummy hanging from a hook next to the waiting area. "What do you think, Doc?"

"I think this makes no sense at all," she said. "This corpse is supposed to be mummified, yet the eyeballs are intact and staring right back at me. At this stage of decomposition, the eyes would certainly be missing due to insects and animals eating them, or they'd be shriveled and dry like the rest of the body."

"I'm glad you're having fun," Burton said. "The fake blood on the walls looks pretty good, though." He got close enough to smell the spattered red mess. "They used a good recipe; a few drops of red food coloring and laundry detergent. I've used it a few times to gross out the Halloween trick-or-treaters."

"Who is next?" the Grim Reaper next to the entrance boomed. He wore a long black cloak and carried a plastic sickle. *"Whose souls will the Realm of Terror claim?"*

"Those would be ours," Burton said, and they all stepped forward.

"Excellent!" the Reaper said through his latex skull mask. "Wait here until I open the dark passageway into the horrifying realm of terror!"

"I think it's going to be dark in there," Gibson said.

"And terrifying," Burton added.

"I don't want to go," said Trellis.

Detective Erin Radley put an arm around him. "It'll be fine, Mike. This kind of fear is fun, because you know you're not in real danger. Your body gets the rush of adrenaline, but you don't have to worry about getting hurt."

"Wrong!" the Reaper bellowed. "He will be torn apart by the cursed beings within the Realm!"

"Guess I was wrong," Radley said. "Sorry, Mike." She looked at the Reaper. "Have you ever thought about doing a study on the effects of fear on people?"

"Silence!" he said.

"No, really," said Radley. "I wonder if this kind of fear

causes people to do things they wouldn't normally do. In real life, when someone is attacked, they sometimes do amazing things to survive. Jump out of windows, break through doors, that kind of thing."

The Reaper looked at her through his black eye holes. "The Realm of Terror will show you the true meaning of fear!"

"Really?" Radley said. "Do you ever have customers fight back and assault the person causing the fear, even though they know it's just someone in a mask?"

The Reaper leaned in close. "Lady, I've been punched, kicked, head-butted, and knocked over by kids half my size. Now what do you say you quit busting my chops and get ready to be scared?"

"This," Radley said, looking at Burton, "is going to be fun."

"Enter the Realm of Terror!" the Reaper said as he pulled the black curtain aside so they could walk through the doorway.

Trellis started muttering, "Oh man oh man oh man . . ."

The first room was supposed to be the lobby of an insane asylum, and a zombie nurse behind the counter said, "Ah, new patients! Will you be staying long?"

"No!" Trellis said.

"Oh, yes, you will!" the nurse yelled and came around the counter with a roaring chain saw. The crew stumbled forward laughing and screaming, with all of the screaming coming from Trellis.

They felt their way through a pitch-black hallway, bumping into one another, the walls, then one another again. They came to a doorway that led into a dungeon room, with shackles and torture devices hanging from the ceiling. Streaks and spatters of blood covered one wall and part of the floor, and Burton watched a horde of flies buzz around the red fluid.

"Hey, let's leave Frank in this room," Radley said. "Maybe he'll develop some manners."

"I have manners," Gibson said. "After I punch someone in the face, I say thank you."

"What are you doing in my dungeon?" the Executioner said, running out from behind them with a large plastic axe above his head.

"We're sealing it off," Burton said, taking his CRIME SEEN? tape out of vest pocket 2. "Someone was assaulted in this room."

How did Burton know?

Burton's File

Blowflies, also called green bottle flies, are attracted to the smell of blood. They feed on it and sometimes lay eggs in it, allowing the hatched larvae to feed on the blood.

The fake blood that the haunted house used was made of red food coloring and detergent, not exactly a recipe that would attract insects. However, the blood in the dungeon room had a swarm of flies around it, indicating that it was real.

The Price of Inflation

Mike Trellis was out of the CSI truck before it stopped moving. He left his door open and ran toward the two-story brick house, yelling, "Don't worry, children! I'm on my way!"

Burton took his time getting out. He saw that his shoelace was a little loose and knelt to retie it. An ant trundled along next to his foot, carrying a piece of food three times its size, and he watched it weave through the blades of grass. Trellis pounded on the front door of the house.

"Crime scene investigators! Open the door immediately!" After about fifteen pounds, a confused woman opened the door.

"Can I help you?" she said.

Trellis said, "We have to get the children out!"

"What? Why?" she said.

"Are you Mrs. Stanton?" Trellis said. "Did I just talk to you on the phone about the birthday party you had here yesterday?"

"Oh, yes," Mrs. Stanton said. "It's a pleasure to meet you."

"Not now," Trellis screeched. "There was a clown in your home yesterday! Get the children outside before it's too late!"

"Oh, my," Mrs. Stanton said. She looked over Trellis's shoulder at Burton, who was walking toward the house twirling his finger next to his head, letting her know not to listen to the crazy person.

"Mrs. Stanton, I'm CSI Wes Burton. This *was* my technician Mike Trellis, but he's obviously gone insane and can no longer perform his duties."

Mrs. Stanton tried to smile. "He mentioned on the phone that you had some questions about the birthday party yesterday."

"Mostly about the entertainment for the party, Jumbles the Clown," Burton said. Trellis had to lean against the door frame to keep himself steady.

"Jumbles?" Mrs. Stanton said. "He didn't do anything wrong while he was here."

"That's good," said Burton. "But after he left, he robbed a video store about three miles from here."

"Goodness," Mrs. Stanton said.

Burton nodded. "He claims he was extremely intoxicated and doesn't remember any of it. The video store was robbed at 3:15 P.M. yesterday, and Jumbles's calendar shows that he was here from 1:00 until 3:00 P.M. Is that correct?"

"Yes, that sounds about right," Mrs. Stanton said.

"If that's the case," Burton said, "and Jumbles was in fact under the influence of alcohol during the robbery, he must have been intoxicated while he was here."

Mrs. Stanton said, "He did smell a little odd, so I suppose he could have been drunk while he was here. How unprofessional."

"You can't trust them," Trellis said, leaning close enough to Mrs. Stanton that she eased the door closed a bit. "They show up with their funny makeup and giant shoes and hop all around yukking it up. Then, when you have your back turned, out come the chain saws!"

"Mike," Burton said. "I think you left something important in the truck."

Trellis wiped sweat from his forehead. "Yeah? What?"

"I don't care, just go find it," Burton said. "Mrs. Stanton, do you mind if I take a look around? There may be some evidence that shows Jumbles was intoxicated while he was here."

"Certainly," Mrs. Stanton said. "So if he was drunk during the robbery, does that mean he isn't guilty?"

"Oh, no," said Burton. "His lawyer is planning on a temporary insanity plea due to the level of alcohol in Jumbles's blood. I don't think they'll pull it off, but if we can determine the blood alcohol level ourselves, we'll know just how drunk he was." Burton moved through the front hall into the kitchen, where a half-eaten birthday cake was covered with plastic wrap.

"Couldn't the arresting officers tell he was drunk?" Mrs. Stanton said.

"Jumbles found a nice pile of garbage to pass out in," said Burton, "and we couldn't find him until this morning. By then, the alcohol was mostly out of his system, and it was too late to give him a Breathalyzer or a blood test." He entered the living room and saw the crumpled piles of wrapping paper and several new toys on the floor. Balloon animals sat on the couch and chairs, looking into the center of the room like an inflatable audience.

"We haven't had a chance to clean up yet," Mrs. Stanton said.

"No, this is good," said Burton. "I'm glad things are as they were yesterday; it's easier to figure out what happened. What's that supposed to be, a giraffe?"

Mrs. Stanton picked up the balloon animal. "I think it's a gopher. Jumbles made these for the kids right before he left. They had all kinds of requests: dog, lion, panda bear, dolphin."

"These animals are all the same species to me," Burton said. "Evidence."

Why are the balloon animals evidence?

Burton's File

When a person drinks alcohol, the body absorbs it into the bloodstream through the mouth, throat, stomach, and intestines. From there, the blood carries it through the body and, as it passes through the lungs, some of the alcohol evaporates into the air that is breathed out. Devices used to determine the amount of alcohol in a person's system, often called Breathalyzers, sample the evaporated alcohol and calculate the amount of alcohol in the person's bloodstream.

Mrs. Stanton said that Jumbles made the balloon animals

just before he left at 3:00 P.M., 15 minutes before he robbed the video store. At that time, his breath would indicate how drunk he was. Using a Breathalyzer test, we can sample the air he blew into the balloons and determine his blood alcohol level just before he committed his crime.

The Shotgun Divorce

Detective Erin Radley was waiting for Burton and Mike Trellis in front of the doctor's office.

"How does it look in there?" Burton asked.

"Messy," said Radley. "Doctor Young is in his office. No one has touched his body or the shotgun, so all the evidence is intact."

"No wonder everyone is scared of shots in this place," Trellis said. "Get it? Because he was a doctor. And he was shot."

"Never speak again," said Burton. The three of them walked through the waiting room and into the hallway that led to Young's office. Burton looked into the small room. Young was tilted back in his office chair, staring at the ceiling. A pump-action shotgun lay across the desk.

"It's good that no one touched the shotgun," Burton said. "Whenever some people see one, they want to pick it up and pump it, to watch the shell fly out of the side. Like in the movies just before a shootout starts."

"I love that sound," said Trellis.

Burton said, "Let's get some video and pictures." Trellis got the video camera running while Burton snapped photographs of the scene.

"See anything yet?" Radley asked from the doorway.

Burton looked away from his camera. "What's the hurry?"

"I made the mistake of giving my cell phone number to Mrs. Young. She's been calling every fifteen minutes for updates."

"Updates?" said Burton. "Like what, if he's still dead?"

"I think she's anxious for us to determine that this was a suicide," Radley said.

"Did she say that?" asked Burton.

"No, but she hinted."

Burton shook his head. "Erin—"

"I know what you're going to say, so save it," Radley said. "You're going to tell me that people lie, what they see isn't always reliable, you don't need the *why* if you can prove the *how*, blah blah blah."

"That's a very good impression," Trellis said.

"You forgot one of my best ones," said Burton. "Evidence is analyzed; testimony is interpreted. Which one do you think is more reliable?"

"Anyway . . ." Radley said.

Burton smiled and looked closely at the entrance wound, then around the room. There weren't any other holes in the walls or furniture. "One shot was fired, and it entered Young's chest. The entrance wound indicates close range, but how close?"

"You mean, close enough for Young to pull the trigger himself?" Radley said.

"Exactly," said Burton. "The shotgun shell was filled with buckshot, so we've got dozens of lead BBs flying at his

194

chest. Generally, buckshot spreads out about an inch for every three feet it travels. If the shotgun was against Young's chest, the entrance wound would just be a big hole. But I see a few little holes around the center, so some of the BBs were spread out when they hit him."

He took a ruler out of vest pocket 13 and held it in front of Young's chest. "Some of the pellets made it almost two inches away from the main entrance wound. Mike, let's get a photo of this."

"One second," Trellis said. "I need to get a good angle on this shotgun shell in the corner." When he was done, he and Burton switched places and Burton knelt next to the shell on the carpet. He gave it a few sniffs, then breathed in deeply; the odor of burnt gunpowder was strong.

"And you call my methods unreliable," said Radley.

"This shell was fired recently," Burton said as he put it in an evidence bag from vest pocket 9. "Since there was only one shot fired in this room, I'd say it's the one that the killer used to murder Young."

How did he know Young was murdered?

Burton's File

There were BBs in Young's chest that had spread almost two inches from the main entrance wound. If buckshot spreads about one inch for every three feet it travels, the gun would have been approximately six feet from Young when it was fired. That's too far for him to pull the trigger himself.

The shotgun was pump-action, and the shell that was fired at Young had fallen from the shotgun, indicating that it had been pumped after Young was shot. If Young shot himself, he couldn't have pumped the shotgun afterward.

The Sole Confession

"I'd guess about a size eleven, maybe eleven-and-a-half," Burton said, holding the right footprint up to the light. He was in the crime lab, sorting through the evidence collected from Benny Erickson's house. Benny had been murdered during the night.

"And you lifted this print off the windowsill?" Detective Erin Radley asked.

"That's right," Burton said. "Benny is a size nine, so it isn't his."

"Why would a murderer go barefoot into a house?" Radley said. "So he could sneak around quietly?"

"From the prints I saw outside the window," Burton said, "it looked like he wore some heavy boots up to the house, then took them off and stepped onto the windowsill to enter the house barefoot."

"Probably so he wouldn't track evidence into the place," Radley said, and Burton nodded. "Can you match the footprint to the person who left it?"

"The print wasn't good enough to get any arches or whorls," Burton said, pointing to the black toe smudges. "So we can't compare them like fingerprints. But studies have shown that the entire footprint may be unique to an individual because of the way that person distributes their weight."

Radley frowned.

"Look at this footprint," Burton said. "You can see the five toes, the ball of the foot here, and then it curves down like a question mark to the heel. You don't see the entire bottom of the foot, because the arch is raised and didn't get pressed onto the windowsill."

"I'm with you," Radley said.

"The studies have shown that no two people put pressure on their feet the exact same way, so this kind of print is unique to one person," said Burton.

Radley nodded. "So all we have to do is find who left this print."

"Right," Burton said. "But there's no official footprint database to compare it to. So we'll have to go around town asking folks to volunteer their feet for a few minutes."

"I'll be on vacation that month," said Radley.

Mike Trellis walked into the lab and stood behind them. They waited for it.

"I sense that the game is afoot," Trellis said. "Get it? Because that's a print of a foot."

Radley put a hand on Trellis's shoulder. "You have problems," she said.

"Mike," Burton said, "did you come in here just to try that joke?"

"No," said Trellis. "I came to let you know that Cedric Rogers is here. He called Benny's answering machine yesterday, threatening to come over and kill Benny."

"I guess Benny didn't check his machine," Burton said,

then turned to Radley. "Is the threat on the answering machine enough to arrest Rogers?"

"We can hold him for 24 hours without a warrant," Radley said, "but unless we can come up with evidence that puts him at the scene, he'll be free to go after that."

"That's exactly what his lawyer said," said Trellis.

"He brought a lawyer?" Burton said.

"Wasn't that rude of him?" said Trellis. "And that's the only thing he *did* say. Rogers isn't going to confess to anything."

Radley said, "It is his right, gentlemen."

"Yeah, but he didn't have to exercise it," Trellis said.

"Did you notice what he was wearing on his feet?" Burton said.

"Some old tennis shoes," said Trellis. "Why?"

"If he had on boots, we could try to match them to the prints outside the window."

Radley said, "If he was smart enough to take those boots off before he went through the window, I doubt he'd be dumb enough to wear them here."

"True," said Burton. "Let's hold him for the 24 hours. When you get his clothes and belongings, bring his shoes down here right away. We're going to need them to get this case to stand up in court."

Why did Burton want the shoes?

Burton's File

Although he didn't realize it, Rogers did bring the CSI team a footprint to compare to the one on the windowsill. The inside of his old tennis shoes would have a perfect pressure imprint of the bottom of his foot, which could then be matched to the one left on Benny's windowsill.

The Truth Was Eating Away at Him

Burton and Mike Trellis cruised through the new housing development.

Trellis said, "Every fourth house is the same."

"Cookie-cutter houses," said Burton. "Your next-door neighbor doesn't have the same house as you, but their next-door neighbor might." He saw the Sensitive Cleaners van parked ahead and slowed to a stop behind it.

"And these lawns," Trellis said. "They look so perfect; I'd feel bad running around on them playing tag."

Burton tried to picture him rolling on the ground, getting dirty and grass-stained. "You never played tag," Burton said.

"Excuse me?" said Trellis. "I was the King of Tag four summers in a row. One time, I wasn't 'it' for seven weeks running." Burton reached over and tapped him on the shoulder.

"You're it," he said and got out of the truck.

"Burtons! Mikes!" Bug said when they got out of the CSI truck. "You drive like syrup going uphill; I've been waiting for days almost."

"Sorry, Bug," said Burton. "Mike had to stop at the store for some hair gel."

"Big date tonight," Trellis said. He reached out and patted Bug on the arm. "You're it."

"Thank you," Bug said. "Mikes, I give you some of my cologne for your date. Is my own recipe."

"Oh, no," said Trellis.

"Yes, is secret formula of lemon juice, crushed red pepper, chocolate sauce, and rubbing alcohol. Women cannot resist."

"Cannot resist what?" Burton said. "Wearing nose plugs?"

"Burtons, that would defeat purpose of fantastic cologne," said Bug.

"Sorry. Which house were you cleaning when you smelled the dead body?"

"This one," Bug said, pointing at the three-story house across the street. It was the only one without a FOR SALE sign on the front lawn. "New owner is moving in next week, and developer asks me to make sure no stains have moved in first. I check all corners and spaces and, when I get to basement, I smell the death."

"Are you sure it wasn't an animal?" Trellis asked.

"Mikes, I have smelled dead animals, and I have smelled dead people. They are not the same."

"He's right," Burton said. "Let's go have a look." The three of them walked toward the house. "I checked my files before we headed out. There's a guy who went missing last week, Bob Warner, who lives a few miles from here. We found traces of his blood at his house, but no body. If someone wanted a private place to store the corpse until they figured out what to do with it, this house would be a pretty good choice."

Trellis said, "If someone's already purchased this house, there wouldn't be any real estate agents coming and going."

"But the killer didn't plan on Bug showing up with his impressive death-detection skills," Bug said.

"Yeah, a criminal never *nose* how we're going to catch them," Trellis said, pointing to his own. "Get it? Because you smelled something."

"Bah ha ha!" Bug laughed and had to sit on the front steps to keep from falling down.

"Good idea, Bug," Burton said. "You wait here while we check the scene. I'd like as few people as possible walking around inside."

"Good, good," Bug said, still chuckling. Burton and Trellis walked into the house, which was all-white walls and beige carpet. They found the basement stairs and started down.

"All I smell is fresh paint and new carpet," said Trellis.

"Enjoy it while you can," Burton said as he walked toward a closed door across the basement. He eased the door open and sampled the air. "There *was* a dead body here recently."

"No kidding," Trellis said through his hand, while he tried to hold his nose closed.

"This window is open a crack," Burton said. "Whoever removed the body probably came and went through there." He approached the window and saw dozens of blowflies clinging to the inside of the glass. "Looks like someone stole your meal, huh, guys?"

"Don't
talk to the insects," Trellis said. "It creeps me out."

"Well, they've been more help than you so far," said Burton. "If there are flies inside the room, they probably laid eggs on the corpse before it was removed. And if they laid eggs," Burton got down on his hands and knees and inspected the carpet, "those eggs probably hatched into larvae that fed on the body."

"Larvae," Trellis said, low. "Just call them by their real name. Maggots."

Burton took a set of tweezers out of vest pocket 24 and evidence bags out of 9. He gently plucked a few half-inch-long maggots from the carpet and placed them in their own bags. "Don't listen to him, my larval friends." He looked at Trellis and whispered, "I have to stay on their good side, because they're going to tell us if it was Bob Warner's body in this room."

How will Burton find out?

Burton's File

Maggots feed on dead tissue, which contains the DNA of the dead body. When the maggots munch on the body, they also consume the DNA.

Traces of Bob Warner's blood were left at his home the day he disappeared and provided a sample of Warner's DNA, which can be compared to the DNA found inside the maggots in the basement.

The Wrong Arm of the Law

"Seriously," Herb Manchester said, sitting in the interview room. "Is this a practical joke?"

"Do I look like a comedian to you?" Detective Frank Gibson said.

"Maybe," said Manchester. "That tie is pretty funny."

"This is no joke, Mr. Manchester," Burton said. "And that tie was a gift from his wife, so she obviously has poor taste in clothing as well as husbands."

"Watch it," Gibson said and turned to Manchester. "I don't see why this is so hard. You've been shot in the arm, and we have the guy who shot you."

"Nobody shot me," Manchester said and held up his left arm, which was bandaged from elbow to shoulder. "I did get shot, yes, but I did it myself, accidentally. I was cleaning my pistol, and it had a round in the chamber. It was a stupid mistake, and I'm lucky to be alive. Who said they shot me?"

Gibson said, "Carl Vincent. Ring a bell?"

"Carl?" Manchester said. "I bet he'd like to shoot me, but I'd never give him the chance."

"You two don't play nice?" said Gibson.

"Not since our business fell apart. I accused him of stealing some of our inventory and selling it on the black market. He said I was just looking for a reason to cut him out of the profits. We're still waiting for the lawyers to sort it all out. Carl and I were supposed to have a one-on-one meeting yesterday, maybe settle the whole mess like professional adults, but I ended up shooting myself. I had to call him and cancel, and I felt like an idiot when I had to explain that I'd put a bullet through my arm. But why would he lie about shooting me?"

"He says you broke down his front door and threatened to kill him," Gibson said. "So he shot you in self-defense."

Manchester's jaw almost fell off. "Now that has to be a joke." Burton and Gibson both shook their heads. "You don't believe him, do you?"

"I believe the evidence," Burton said as he pulled out the photographs of Manchester's bullet wound that had been taken in the emergency room the day before. "I can tell by the photos that the bullet entered your left biceps area and exited the back of your arm at a slight upward angle. So you were holding the gun with your right hand and cleaning it with your left?"

"That's right," Manchester said. "I reached for the gun oil with my left and must have squeezed the trigger with my right thumb."

"So you're denying his claims?" said Gibson.

"Absolutely," Manchester said. "He's obviously trying to make me look like a lunatic so the court will decide in his favor."

"'Obvious' can be a dirty word around here," said Burton. "If we learn something, it could be because someone wants it that way."

"Oh, come on," Manchester said, looking at the two of them for a sign that they were kidding. Gibson smiled with all his teeth, and Burton was busy looking at the other photos in the case file. There were shots of Carl Vincent's front door from all angles; Mike Trellis had done a fantastic job capturing every detail of the entryway. There were several images from inside the house looking out through the broken door. The bullet hole on the left side of the door frame was labeled 9 MILLIMETER, the same size bullet that had gone through Manchester's arm.

"I'm going to have a few words with Mr. Vincent," Burton said.

"Carl's here right now?" said Manchester, jumping out of his seat. "Let me talk to him, we'll get this straightened out right now."

"Sit down and shut your trap," Gibson said. Manchester did both.

In another interview room, Burton took a chair across from Carl Vincent. "Let's go through it one more time, Mr. Vincent."

"Is Herb here yet?" Vincent said. "You're not going to let him see me, are you? Because he's nuts!"

"Take it easy," said Burton. "You're perfectly safe. Now please, tell me what happened."

"Okay," Vincent said. "I was watching television and heard a car pull into the driveway. I got up to see who it was, but before I could get to the door it crashed in, and Herb was standing there, screaming that he was going to kill me. Ever since our business went bad, Herb's been acting weird, so I started carrying a pistol. And, like I told you before, I have a permit. So I pulled it out and fired and hit Herb. It all happened so fast. I didn't think I'd be able to shoot someone face-to-face like that, looking right into their eyes."

"How close was Mr. Manchester when you fired?" Burton asked. He could tell from the on-scene bullet path analysis, but he wanted to hear what Vincent would say.

"Let's see, I was near the end of the hall, and Herb was just inside the door, so . . . 8 feet?"

Burton said, "My tests show you fired from 7 feet, 10 inches, so you were almost right. If Mr. Manchester *had* been standing there, you would have shot him. But he wasn't."

How did Burton know Carl Vincent was lying?

Burton's File

Looking out Carl Vincent's doorway from the hall, the bullet hole was on the left side of the door frame. Herb Manchester's bullet wound was on his upper left arm, entering the biceps and exiting out the back of his arm. Vincent claimed that Manchester was just inside the door when he shot him, while looking into his eyes. If that were true, the bullet hole would be on the right side of the door frame, not the left.

Wild Noose Chase

Burton, Mike Trellis, and Dr. Lauren Crown were in the crime lab making sure everything was ready for the special autopsy.

"Isn't it nice in here?" Burton said. "Quiet, professional, everyone just doing their job and —"

Detective Frank Gibson burst through the double doors, escorting a small man. He said, "This is Philip Waterfield. He's . . . what do you do again?"

"I'm the president of the Council to Preserve Local History," Waterfield said.

"CPLH," Gibson said to himself. "You should come up with a better name. Something that spells a cool word, like HOTT or GUNS."

"You mean an acronym?" said Waterfield.

Gibson looked at him like he was crazy. "That's not a cool word," he said, and walked over to look at the skeleton on the examination table. "So, this is our famous outlaw, huh?"

Trellis said, "I call him Killy the Dead. Get it? Instead of Billy the Kid."

"Frank," Burton said, "meet Nathanial Treadbare, horse thief, gunslinger, and all-around bad guy. He robbed a train in February 1872, was arrested in April, and hanged in May."

"Ah, the good old days," Gibson said.

"Let's not get ahead of ourselves, Mr. Burton," Waterfield said. "We don't know for sure that he was hanged, remember?"

"Uh-oh," said Gibson. "Looks like the brainiacs are going to have an argument. Five bucks on the little guy, Crown, what do you say?" Dr. Crown didn't look up from her stainless steel tools. "All right, never mind her. Five bucks on both of you."

"We're not arguing, Frank," said Burton. "The historical records show Treadbare was hanged on May 12, 1872. And from the time of his arrest to the time of the hanging, he was too drunk to stand up or talk to anyone. He had to be carried to the gallows. Rumors started that he may have already been dead, but the lawmen wanted the glory for catching him alive, so they staged the hanging. Mr. Waterfield and the Council requested that we exhume the body to see which is true, the history or the rumors."

"As Mr. Burton mentioned," Waterfield said, "Mr. Treadbare avoided capture for two months after the train robbery." He sounded like he was proud.

"Yeah?" Gibson said as he looked the corpse up and down. "I'd have caught him sooner."

"I brought a picture of him that is dated a few days before he was caught," said Waterfield. He carefully opened his binder and showed the yellowed photograph of Treadbare standing next to a horse, his six-gun hanging low on his right hip.

"Nice gun," Gibson said.

Waterfield nodded. "He didn't get a chance to fire it when he was arrested. They caught him in an outhouse."

"And he was already dead?" said Gibson.

"That's what I'm here to find out," said Waterfield.

"Well, I've been in an outhouse before," Gibson said,

"and they were probably ten times worse back then. I'd have picked death, too."

"I think we're ready," Burton said to Waterfield. "The advanced state of decomposition might make it difficult to find out how he died, but if there is any proof, we'll find it."

While Trellis took photos and video of the body, Burton said, "Now, there are two ways to die from hanging. If the drop is far enough, the rope will break the victim's neck and kill them almost instantly." He snapped his fingers and Waterfield jumped. Gibson laughed.

"Unless the drop is too far," Trellis said. "Then the head comes right off like a cork. Pop!" Waterfield looked around for a chair.

"That's true," Burton said. "But I think you'd rather have that than a rope that's too short. If the drop isn't far enough to break the neck, the victim dies from lack of oxygen, and it's much slower."

Waterfield glanced at the corpse. "Do you think that's what happened to Treadbare?" he said.

"We took some X-rays before bringing the body out here," said Burton. "They showed no fractures in the neck vertebrae. That means, if he was hanged, they didn't drop him far enough to break his neck."

"Goodness," said Waterfield.

Burton said, "But something else caught my eye in the X-rays." He picked up a tape measure from the stainless steel cart next to the table. "I wanted to wait until you arrived before I verified it. Let's start with the right arm. I'm going to measure from the top of the humerus to the end of the radius and ulna."

Burton touched the end of the measuring tape to the skeleton's right shoulder socket and brought it down to the right wrist.

"Measures 20 inches," said Burton. "Now we'll do the left arm . . . 20 inches and three eighths. That puts the left arm at nearly a half inch longer than the right."

"Okay," Waterfield said.

"So what?" Gibson added.

"You're right-handed, correct?" Burton said.

"Yeah," said Gibson. "Again, so what?"

Burton said, "I'll bet if I measured your arm bones, your right side would be a bit longer than your left. It's from constantly using your right hand to reach for things, carry things, everyday tasks that stretch your bones."

Waterfield looked at the skeleton. "So, you think this skeleton was left-handed?"

"That's right," Burton said. "And that it isn't Nathanial Treadbare."

Why not?

Burton's File

In the photograph Waterfield brought, Nathanial Treadbare is standing with his gun on his right hip. If the gun is on his right hip, then he must be right-handed.

Wine and Die

It was almost midnight when Mike Trellis stuck his head into the crime lab and turned off the lights.

"Hey!" Burton yelled from somewhere in the darkness.

"Whoops," Trellis said, and turned the lights back on. "I thought I was the only one here."

"He's so self-centered," Burton said to Dr. Crown, who was getting back to work now that she could see again. Burton turned to Trellis. "We're still working on Vincent Sanders, the guy they found in the park this afternoon."

"The dead guy?" Trellis said, walking over.

"No, he's still alive," Burton said. "It makes the autopsy difficult at first, but you get used to it."

"Wouldn't that be more like an ow-topsy?" Trellis said. "Get it? Ow-topsy?"

Burton picked up a bone saw. "Get on the table," he said.

"I need that," Dr. Crown said and took the saw. "I'm almost through the skull."

"Fantastic," said Burton.

"What did you find so far?" Trellis asked.

"We know the cause of death was a stab wound to the chest," Burton said, then lowered his voice. "But because of environmental factors, we don't know the time of death."

"I can hear you," Dr. Crown said as she gently put the bone saw down. "And I will determine the time of death. It's just going to take longer than usual."

Trellis said, "Well, 'usual' is about five seconds for you, so I think we're into record-setting territory here." Dr. Crown picked up a cranium chisel, and Trellis stepped behind Burton. "But enough about all that," he said. "What do you expect to find inside the skull?"

"We swabbed the mouth and nose," said Burton, "looking for traces of dirt, pollen, something that would show Sanders was alive and breathing when he was at the park. We didn't find any of that, so it looks like his body was dumped at the park. But we did find red wine in his nose."

"Wine?" Trellis said.

"We talked to Jenny Sanders, who had lunch with her husband today," said Burton. "She says the last she saw of Vincent, he was getting into his car to go back to work. We checked her car and found a bottle of red wine and compared a sample of it to the swab from Vincent's nose. It matched."

"Okay," Trellis said. "But why was it in his nose?"

"I'm into the nasal passage," Crown said, and Burton turned back to the examination table.

He said, "Let's swab it and see if we're on the right track."

"What track?" Trellis said. "I hate it when I'm left out."

Dr. Crown looked at him.

"Uh-oh," Burton said. "Get ready for your anatomy lesson."

"Press your tongue against the roof of your mouth," Dr. Crown said. "That's your hard palate. Keeping the terms simple, it separates your mouth from your nose. Now, move your tongue back until your find a soft spot." Burton and Trellis both did it, their chins stretching out like they had peanut butter stuck in their mouths.

"That's your soft palate," Dr. Crown said. "And behind that is where your nasal cavity drains into your throat."

"Gross," Trellis said, but it didn't sound right because he still had his tongue pressed against his soft palate.

"When you swallow," Dr. Crown said, "your soft palate moves back and closes off the passage to your nasal cavity. This keeps food and liquid from entering your nose. However, when you laugh, the soft palate leaves the passage open."

"I think I see where this is going," Trellis said.

Dr. Crown nodded. "If you laugh while you're swallowing, the soft palate gets mixed messages. Should it open or close? If it opens, whatever is in your mouth will shoot through your nose."

"Like what happened to you at lunch just last week," Burton said.

"Oh, yeah," Trellis said. "I made that amazingly funny joke about the ham sandwich and the lettuce. Remember?"

"I remember you spraying soda out of your nose," Burton said, "and crying about it for an hour because it hurt so much."

"It did," said Trellis. "It stung like crazy."

"Lucky for you," Dr. Crown said, "the body cleans the nasal passages constantly and gets rid of any irritants right away."

"So you think that's what happened to Vincent?" Trellis

said.

"He had wine at lunch and sprayed some through his nose?"

"We're about to find out," Burton said. Dr. Crown swabbed the body's nasal cavity and tested the residue.

"We have a match," she said. "The wine in the nasal cavity matches the wine Jenny and Vincent had for lunch."

"So Jenny must be pretty funny," Trellis said, "making him shoot wine through his nose like that."

Burton said, "I'll bet she was hilarious. Right up until she killed him."

How did he know?

Burton's File

As Dr. Crown said, the nasal passage is constantly being cleaned by the body, removing irritating objects and substances from the area. If Vincent still had wine in his nasal passage when he was killed, he had to have been murdered almost immediately after he shot wine through his nose. The only person present at that time was his wife, Jenny.

Glossary

Abrasion — When skin is worn or rubbed away.

Accelerant — A flammable material used to start a fire.

Adipocere — The fatty, waxlike substance that forms on a dead body when water is involved.

Asphyxiate — To die from a lack of oxygen to the brain.

Autopsy — The examination of a corpse to determine or confirm the cause of death.

Blood spatter — The pattern of blood deposits at a crime scene that can help determine what occurred at the scene.

Compress — To press or squeeze.

Convict — **n.** A person found guilty of an offense or crime. **v.** To prove someone guilty of a crime in court.

Cranium — The skull.

Cyanoacrylate — Also known as superglue, it is fumed over substances to reveal fingerprints.

Deceased — A body that is no longer living.

Decompose — When a body starts to decay or break down after death.

DNA — The molecule that carries the genetic information in the cell. Traces of DNA from saliva, skin, blood, and other sources can be used to identify the person who left the trace.

EMT — Emergency medical technician.

Evidence — Any physical item that assists in proving or disproving a conclusion. For example, a paint scraping is evidence; an eyewitness account is not.

Flourescein — A fluorescent chemical that is sprayed on an area and viewed under ultraviolet light. It will make bloodstains glow in the dark. Flourescein can expose blood on surfaces that have been cleaned with bleach, but not on surfaces that have been painted over. For that, you will need *luminol*.

Gas chromatograph/mass spectrometer (GC/MS) — A system of instruments used to separate a complex mixture and identify its components.

Glucose — The main circulating sugar in the blood and the major energy source of the body.

GSR — Gunshot residue, the trace materials left behind when a gun is fired.

Hemorrhage — A rapid and sudden loss of blood.

Homicide — The killing of one person by another.

Hypoglycemia — An abnormally low level of glucose in the blood.

Laceration — A jagged wound or cut.

Lividity — The discoloration of the skin caused by the settling of blood that occurs in a body after the heart stops.

Luminol — a fluorescent chemical that is sprayed on an area and viewed under ultraviolet light. It will make bloodstains glow in the dark. Luminol can even expose blood on surfaces that have been painted over, but not on surfaces that have been cleaned with bleach. For that, you will need *fluorescein*.

Marbled — Patterned with veins or streaks of color resembling marble.

Postmortem — Occurring after death.

Silver latent print powder — A fine dust used to reveal prints (finger, hand, ear, etc.) at a crime scene. After the prints are dusted and photographed, they can be preserved and catalogued with lifting tapes.

Stippling — The deposit of unburned powder and other gunshot residue on a bullet wound. It can help determine the distance between the shooter and the victim.

Toxicology — The analysis of poisons and drugs in the blood and body fluids.

Trace element — A very small bit of chemicals or evidence.

Trajectory — The path of an object moving through the air.

UV light — Ultraviolet light, also known as black light, is used to identify many trace evidence items such as body fluids, drugs, and inks.

About the Author

Jeremy Brown resides in Kalamazoo, Michigan, and at various times in his life thought he was a professional wrestler, a ninja, a werewolf, and Batman, all of which were untrue. He spends his time writing, reading, and designing and operating a haunted house. He hasn't given up on the werewolf thing just yet.